He could give the... dark and danger...

And those eyes were exactly the color of chocolate syrup. Not to mention the eyelashes to die for. What was a man doing with eyelashes like that? And if she could keep babbling long enough, maybe Christian wouldn't kiss her, because if he did she was toast.

Lolly was so close she could see the flecks of gold in his eyes and hear the hitch in his breathing. At least this was affecting him as much as it was affecting her. She knew kissing him had to be a terrible mistake, but her body said something different. Lolly tilted her chin and opened her mouth just as he put his lips to hers.

At first it was soft and gentle, but like a match running slow motion across sandpaper, the sparks ignited a fire of passion, lust, hormones— heavens above, she didn't know what it was, but it was hot!

He threaded his fingers through her hair and held her as if he thought she was going somewhere. No way! She'd never been kissed like this before. It was better than the Fourth of July fireworks. It was a banana split, size eight bathing suit, first kiss kind of wonderful!

Hi, y'all,

Reading's like a minivacation without the hassle. It's a perfect way to avoid airport lineups and cranky kids in a minivan. If you can add a tropical beach or a cozy fire on a hot-chocolate day, it's even better.

I had so much fun immersing myself in the life of Port Serenity. As I was growing up in a small south Texas town, I enjoyed a host of eccentric and colorful friends, neighbors and relatives. The influences of my childhood provided me with the wonderful cast of sassy and sometimes unpredictable citizens in this book.

When bodies start washing up on the Gulf beach, Police Chief Lolly LaTullipe's world is turned upside down. She's sexy, blond and a single mom, and these aren't ordinary bodies—they belong to the bad guys of the Houston drug world.

Enter Christian Delacroix, a dark and dangerous undercover narcotics cop, and you can bet there'll be sparks. As Lolly and Christian deal with the problems and joys associated with the folks of this beach community, they discover the best of all possible worlds—true love.

So find an easy chair and visit Port Serenity, where life is anything but serene!

Happy reading,

Ann DeFee

P.S. I'd love to hear from readers. You can reach me at P.O. Box 97313, Tacoma, WA 98497-0313. Or e-mail me at: ann@ann-defee.com.

A
Texas State
of Mind
Ann DeFee

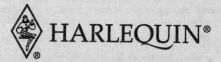

HARLEQUIN®

TORONTO • NEW YORK • LONDON
AMSTERDAM • PARIS • SYDNEY • HAMBURG
STOCKHOLM • ATHENS • TOKYO • MILAN • MADRID
PRAGUE • WARSAW • BUDAPEST • AUCKLAND

ISBN 0-373-75080-3

A TEXAS STATE OF MIND

www.eHarlequin.com

Printed in U.S.A.

A huge thanks to some people who made this possible.
Kay Austin, my critique partner and good friend.
How many times did you read this story?
Paula Eykelhof, the best editor a writer could want.
Thanks for hanging in there with me.
Miriam Kriss—what an agent!
And Debbie Macomber, a terrific fairy godmother.

Chapter One

Oooh, boy! Lolly raised her Pepsi in a tribute to Meg Ryan. Could that girl fake the big O! Lord knows Lolly had perfected the very same skill before Wendell, her ex, hightailed it out to Vegas to find fame and fortune as a drummer. Good old Wendell—more frog than prince. But to give credit where credit was due, he'd managed to sire two of the most fantastic kids in the world.

Nowadays she didn't have to worry about Wendell's flagging ego, or for that matter, any of his other wilting body parts. Celibacy had some rewards. Not many, but a few.

Meg had just segued from the throes of parodied passion to a big smile when Lolly's cell phone rang.

"Great, just great," Lolly muttered. She thumped her Pepsi on the coffee table.

"Chief, I hate to call you at suppertime, but I figured you'd want to handle this one. I just got a call from Bud out at the Peaceful Cove Inn, and he's got hisself something of a problem." An eight o'clock call from the Port Serenity Police Department's gravel-voiced night dispatcher signaled the end to her evening of popcorn and chick flicks.

Chief of Police Lavinia "Lolly" Lee Hamilton La-Tullipe sighed. Her hectic life as a single mom and head of a small police force left her very little free time, and when she had a few moments she wanted to spend them at home with Amanda and Bren, not out corralling scumbags.

"Cletus is on duty tonight, and that man can handle anything short of a full-scale riot," Lolly argued, even though she knew her objections were futile.

Lordy. She'd rather eat Aunt Sissy's fruitcake than abandon the comfort of her living room, especially when Meg was about to find Mr. Right. Lolly hadn't even been able to find Mr. Sorta Right, although she'd given it the old college try. Wendell looked pretty good on the outside, but inside he was like an overripe watermelon—mushy and tasteless. Too bad she hadn't noticed that shortcoming when they started dating in high school. Back then his antics were cute; at thirty-seven they weren't quite so appealing. Good thing he'd been gone for almost eight years.

"I'd really rather not go out tonight."

"Yes, ma'am. I understand. But this one involves Precious." The dispatcher chuckled when Lolly groaned.

Precious was anything but precious. She was the seventeen-year-old demon daughter of Mayor Lance Barton, Lolly's boss and a total klutz in the single-dad department. She and Lance had been buddies since kindergarten, so without a doubt she'd be making an unwanted trip to the Peaceful Cove Inn.

"Oh, man. What did I do to deserve that brat in my life?" Lolly rubbed her forehead in a vain attempt to ward off the headache she knew was coming. "Okay, what's she done now?"

"Seems she's out there with some guys Bud don't know, and she's got a snoot full. He figured we'd want to get her home before someone saw her."

Lolly resisted a sigh. "All right, I'll run out and see what I can do. Call her daddy and tell him what's happening."

She muttered an expletive as she marched to the rolltop desk in the kitchen to retrieve her bag, almost tripping over Harvey, the family's gigantic mutt. She strapped on an ankle holster and then checked her Taser and handcuffs. In this business, a girl had to be prepared.

Amanda, her ten-year-old daughter, was immersed in homework, and as usual, her fourteen-year-old son had his head inside the refrigerator.

"Bren, get Amanda to help you with the kitchen." Lolly stopped him as he tried to sneak out of the room and motioned at the open dishwasher and pile of dishes in the sink. "I've got to go out for a few minutes. If you need anything call your Mee Maw."

Her firstborn rolled his eyes. "Aw, Mom."

Lolly suppressed the urge to laugh, and instead employed the dreaded raised eyebrow. The kid was in dire need of a positive male role model. Someone stable, upright, respectable and…safe. Yeah, safe. It was time to find a reliable, dependable prince—an orthodontist might be nice, considering Amanda's overbite.

"I'm leaving. You guys be good," Lolly called out as she opened the screen door.

A KALEIDOSCOPE OF COLOR from the garish neon beer signs reflected off puddles in the pitted asphalt. What a dump! Lolly parked her police Blazer and checked out the current clientele of Port Serenity's most infamous dive. A couple of Bubba pickups, a red Mustang convertible and a shiny chrome Harley—nothing that sent up immediate red flags. Nevertheless, she patted her purse, ready for any situation.

Describing the Peaceful Cove as an inn was akin to calling a whorehouse a ladies' knitting club. With its peeling paint and plastic sign hanging at half-mast, it was, in fact, a hole-in-the wall eyesore, and redneck central for Lolly's little part of the Texas Gulf Coast. For years, Port Serenity's city fathers had been trying to get rid of the place. A category-four hurricane would probably be the only thing that would actually do the trick.

When Lolly stepped inside, she was almost bowled over by the noxious odor of stale beer, cigarette smoke and sweat. As she did a quick reconnaissance of the room, she noticed a man and woman engrossed in a pool game and two men sitting at a table in the shadows. A hoot of laughter came from the booth in the corner where Precious and her friends were holding court.

Lolly glanced at the problem kids before she strolled over to the bar to talk to a grizzled old man halfheartedly wiping the wooden surface. "Hey, Bud, I heard you called." She avoided looking at the filthy rag in his hand. Her gag reflex was alive and well, thank you. "They been giving you a hard time, or are you just trying to keep from having trouble?" Lolly nodded over her shoulder.

"Don't want the mayor on my butt. I wouldn't serve 'em nothing, 'cause if those girls ain't underage, my old coon dog's a squirrel. Then them boys got lippy. The only reason they backed off was that mean-looking son-of-a-gun in the black T-shirt told 'em to sit down and shut up. Guess they didn't want to take him on." Bud chuckled. "Even those sissy college boys ain't that stupid."

Lolly studied the man in question. Bud had nailed him to a T. With the physique of a pro linebacker and a slicked-back ponytail the color of midnight, he was a poster child for *America's Most Wanted.*

Nope—this one wasn't a choirboy, and he was watching her like a mountain lion eying his prey. Ooh, yeah, she'd have big trouble on her hands if he realized she was a police officer. So she'd make sure he didn't.

"Pour me five Cokes, and I'll get rid of the brats for you." Lolly winked at Bud and took another peek at the man in the shadows.

CHRISTIAN DELACROIX WAS bored. He was fed up with his life, his job as an undercover cop for the Texas Department of Safety, Narcotics Division, and with swilling warm beer waiting for a sleazy informant to show up. As far as he was concerned the Houston drug dealers could kill each other off, and he'd stand back and applaud. Unfortunately, this backwater town was the key to his current investigation.

Another burst of laughter distracted him. What he wouldn't give to teach those frat boys a few manners. But if he acted on that impulse, he'd be up to his hubcaps in paperwork, and paperwork was the last thing he needed.

What he really wanted to do was settle down with a good woman. His current fantasy included a picket fence, a couple of kids and a golden retriever. Fat chance! Not with *his* job. But there was light at the end of the tunnel—the minute he finished this assignment, he was going to make some major changes, both professionally and personally.

So Christian brooded and watched the entrance while

C. J. Baker, his friend and fellow undercover narc, leaned his chair back on two legs and popped his gum in perfect rhythm to an old Billy Ray Cyrus tune. Snap, crackle, pop. Snap, snap, crackle, pop, pop. Christian gritted his teeth on the last series of pops.

"Man, oh, man, would you look at that," Christian muttered as he eyed a voluptuous blond Amazon in the doorway. Curvy enough to fulfill any man's fantasy, her luscious hips were encased in a pair of skintight jeans. Christian blinked. She had to be a hallucination created by his sex-starved libido.

He barely resisted the urge to whack himself upside the head. He was looking for Marion the Librarian, not Marilyn Monroe. And this was Marilyn Monroe and Pamela Anderson all wrapped up in one mouthwatering package.

"Oh, man." Christian's heartfelt mumble prompted his companion to quit popping his gum. Those jeans and that sexy saunter should be illegal, or at the very least stamped with a "hazardous to your health" disclaimer.

"Boy, she seems familiar." C.J. rubbed the back of his neck. "I'm sure I know her from somewhere."

"In your dreams, kid."

"No, I know her. Just give me a few minutes and I'll remember." C.J. slammed all four legs of the chair on the floor and stared.

"Don't strain yourself, kid. It'll give you hemorrhoids." Christian couldn't take his eyes off the blonde, even though in his business a distraction could be deadly.

C.J. tapped his fingers on his forehead. "It's coming, it's coming."

"Yeah, sure," Christian said, but all his attention was

centered on Blondie at the bar. After a short conversation she hefted a tray of drinks and strolled toward the raucous kids.

"Why do you think she's still toting that purse?" C.J. asked. "It's as big as a suitcase."

Christian was wondering the same thing. "She's probably afraid the old geezer will steal her wallet." He chuckled when she plopped the tray on the kids' table with a crash.

"Oh, my God! I can't believe it," C.J. yelped. "That's Lolly Hamilton! She sure didn't look like *that* when we were in high school. She was stick-skinny, all legs and elbows. And she had thick glasses, too."

"Well, she's not stick-skinny now." And that, Christian thought, was the understatement of the century.

The ringleader of the college crowd produced a cell phone and drew a nod of approval from Blondie. She listened to the phone conversation for a few minutes and apparently felt confident that the problem was solved because she turned and headed for the bar.

"She might not recognize me. We didn't exactly run in the same crowd," C.J. said. "Lolly was a bookworm and I was kind of wild."

"Oh, really," Christian scoffed. "I have a hard time believing she was ever a wallflower. But you're still a wild man." He took a pull on his beer while he enjoyed her attributes—until she stopped dead in her tracks, stared at C.J. and then broke into a million-dollar smile.

"Cookie Baker! Oh, my land. I can't believe it's you."

"Did she just call you *Cookie* Baker?" Christian's comment elicited a scowl from the blond beauty. Why was she glaring at him, and where was that wonderful smile?

"Last thing I heard, you were a Marine. Are you still in the military?" she asked C.J., deliberately ignoring Christian.

C.J. grinned and tipped his chair back. "Nope. I got out a while ago."

"Yeah, my friend here isn't exactly the military type." Christian felt compelled to join the conversation, even though he hadn't been invited. There was something about the woman that got under his skin.

Then she turned her back on him. Well, if that didn't fry him to a crisp. What had he done to warrant the cold shoulder? Nothing, absolutely nothing! Still, he couldn't believe what he was considering. It had to be the devil on his shoulder. That sucker always got him in a mess of trouble. But trouble or no trouble, he was about to teach this delectable little morsel a lesson on hospitality, Texas style.

It was a huge mistake, he'd be the first to admit it, but he couldn't help himself. Without a word, Christian put his arm around her waist and jerked the blond bombshell into his lap.

LORDY MERCY! Lolly couldn't believe she'd pulled such a brainless stunt. Even as a rookie she'd known better than to turn her back on a guy like him. Stupid! Stupid! Stupid!

Now she was plunked on his lap with his arms planting her firmly in place. Not only that, he had the nerve to be nuzzling the sensitive skin of her neck with his five-o'clock stubble. Sure, the guy was grade-A sex on the hoof—whew, she mentally fanned herself just thinking about it—but he probably had a rap sheet a mile long. Tarnation!

Lolly reached into her purse, flipped on her stun gun and silently counted to ten waiting for it to charge. She told herself that was the reason she let him snuggle those few extra moments. Then she pulled out of his grip and smiled. "Sugar, I think you need to learn some manners."

He fell like a giant redwood when she zapped his bare arm with the 65,000 volts.

Chapter Two

Lolly tried in vain to ignore the queasy feeling in her stomach as she listened to Sergeant Joe's recitation of the previous evening's blotter. It had been a slow night in Port Serenity—a couple of kids partying at the quay and a domestic at the trailer park. Those incidents didn't compare to her encounter at the Peaceful Cove Inn.

What in the world had possessed her to stun the guy? She was a professional law enforcement officer; she could've handled him another way. Despite the fact that he had his hands all over her, Lolly hadn't been frightened. Irritated and more than a bit aroused—heavens above, where had *that* come from? But she'd never been scared.

She could've flipped out her badge and put him in his place. But no! What did the hotshot police chief do? She zapped his butt and left him on the grimy floor for C.J. to deal with. No doubt about it, she was gutless.

Lolly smiled. She shouldn't have done it, but the look on C.J.'s face when his friend crashed to the floor had been priceless. And it *had* put the fear of God into the rowdy college kids. They'd turned into instant mush when he'd crumpled in a heap. But all in all, she still felt bad. Really bad.

"Chief, have you heard a word I've said?"

Oops. Busted. "Sorry, Joe. I didn't quite catch everything." Lolly hoped that would be enough of a concession for her second-in-command.

"Now, there's an understatement. I just told you we budgeted fifty thousand for the department picnic next week, and you didn't bat an eyelash. You might as well tell me what's got you so distracted, because you know I'm gonna pester you until I find out."

Coming from him, that wasn't an idle threat. Joe Hawkins was a tenacious cop. He was also a good friend. But she wasn't about to spill her guts concerning last night's fiasco. Hopefully, she'd heard the end of it.

"Sorry." Lolly shrugged. "I have a few things on my mind." Try as she might, she couldn't get that rugged specimen of manhood out of her mind. He wasn't handsome but oh, my—was he sexy.

Lolly suppressed a groan. Sexy and rugged were not words permitted in her vocabulary *or* her fantasies.

"And we had a break-in at the Senior Center." Joe thumbed through his notes until he found the page he wanted. "The perps took three cases of Chef Boyardee and the bingo machine."

"Bingo machine?"

"Yeah, you know—it pops up numbers like popcorn? B-16." He mimicked using a microphone to call a bingo number.

Lolly laughed. "Let's hope the Catholic ladies don't do a spaghetti-and-bingo night anytime soon. I'd hate to have to bust Father Don."

Joe nodded and rolled his ever-present toothpick

around in his mouth. "And last but not least...Peach-tree has made his summer move out to the Point. He's using one of the sheds at the old quarry."

Peachtree was the town eccentric who'd been around for as long as Lolly could remember. He wore flowing robes and held impromptu revival meetings anyplace he could corral two or more people.

During the winter months he made camp under the causeway bridge, and in the summer he moved closer to the water. The town's Good Samaritans had tried in vain to get him into a proper house, but he always refused. He said he was closer to God out under the stars.

"Have someone check on him periodically," Lolly instructed. The man was harmless, and he *was* the closest thing the town had to a troll under the bridge.

A young patrolman stuck his head in the door. "Chief, hate to break in on your meeting, but Charlie called and said Peachtree's found a dead guy on the beach." He waited while Lolly and Joe absorbed the news.

Lolly put her head in her hands. "Not another one." It was the second body in as many weeks. Crimes like murder didn't happen in Port Serenity. Their town was known for Victorian cottages, bed-and-breakfasts, bird sanctuaries and expensive waterfront homes. Not dead bodies!

People rarely locked their doors, and kids played in the streets. Sure, they had their share of tourists, but most of the wild ones went out to the island to romp in the Gulf surf. Bird watchers in Bermuda shorts were more the order of the day. Nope, this wasn't *supposed* to happen in Port Serenity.

"Tell him we'll be out there in ten minutes and call Olivia to let her know." Olivia Alvarado was Lolly's best friend. She also happened to be the county coroner.

"Dr. Olivia's already out there. She saw Charlie's lights and followed him." The young rookie lowered his voice. "She said to tell you she thinks it's another frozen body."

Oh, great! Just what Lolly needed—a serial killer whipping up Homo sapiens Popsicles.

"Was it a whole body or was it body parts?" Lolly asked, even though she wasn't sure she wanted to know.

The kid rubbed his head. "I think it was a whole body."

Lolly reached into the desk for her bottle of Tylenol. "Good. I *hate* parts."

"Should I go with you?" the young patrolman asked.

He reminded her so much of an eager puppy she wanted to protect his innocence a little longer. "No, not this time." She turned to Joe. "Ready?"

"Yep."

"I have to talk to one of the detectives. Then I'll go by my office and get my holster. Meet you out back." But before Lolly could make it out the door, her administrative assistant, Dora, waved at her to stop. "There are two guys who insist on seeing you. They're real adamant about waiting in your office."

"Do you think they're armed?" Lolly didn't have time for this.

"Nope. But one of 'em looks like he could be a tackle for the Cowboys. I don't think he'd need a weapon. And the other one's real familiar."

Lolly shook her head. "Joe and I have to go to a crime scene. I don't know when we'll be back. Tell them to leave a number and I'll call them and make an appointment."

Dora seemed skeptical but went off to deliver the message.

"What was that all about?" Joe asked.

Lolly raised an eyebrow. "Beats me, but I guess I'll find out." The only football player she'd seen lately was the guy from the Peaceful Cove, and Lolly would bet her bottom dollar he wouldn't show up at a police station. Not unless he was wearing a shiny pair of handcuffs.

CHRISTIAN GROUND his teeth. This was a stupid idea. He knew beyond the shadow of a doubt that he was going out on a limb, but he wasn't about to let some blond bimbo get away with using a stun gun on him. She might be Marilyn Monroe incarnate, but that didn't give her license to fry his circuits. And what was she doing with a Taser anyway?

Until his personal encounter with that one last night, he hadn't realized just how bad the thing hurt. He still ached, from the top of his head to the tips of his toes.

C.J. grinned and popped his gum. "This is really dumb. You know that, don't you?"

When C.J. was right—he was right. Undercover cops didn't hang out at police stations, but Christian was beginning to suspect his cover didn't matter, anyway. This whole investigation was feeling like a big fat zero.

Christian scowled at his partner. Why had he let the twit come with him? "You know what, *Cookie?* I don't give a flying fig what you think. We're up to our eyebrows in dog poop, and I don't see things improving. All we know for sure is that Sean Gomez washed ashore, dead as a mackerel, right here in good old Port Serenity." Christian scrubbed his face with one hand.

"We've been in this backwater for almost three weeks, and what do we have to show for it? Except for the bedbugs in that dumpy apartment I'm renting, we have nada, nothing, zippo, zilch. And furthermore, I never want to see a shrimp again as long as I live." Christian had spent his undercover time unloading commercial fishing boats while C.J. hung around the pool hall. Wrestling with smelly seafood was not what he'd envisioned when he was promoted to Lieutenant. "Next time, I'll kick back and drink beer, and you can do the heavy lifting."

C.J. flashed Christian his best boyish grin. "At least you're not staying at the roach motel. And by the way, if you call me Cookie again, I'm going to rearrange that pretty face of yours." The charm C.J. could conjure up so easily was a convenient mask for a ruthlessly shrewd mind. That innocent expression was one of the reasons C.J. was such a good narc cop. Who would ever suspect the Beaver? Christian, on the other hand, looked like he chewed rusty nails for breakfast.

The word on the mean streets of Houston was that something big was happening in Port Serenity, and since C.J. was familiar with the area, they'd been assigned to investigate. But the only lead they had was a dead Houston drug dealer who'd washed ashore with his driver's license stapled to his shirt and a sealed bag of cocaine around his neck.

"Too bad the guy we were supposed to meet last night flaked out." C.J. snapped his gum for emphasis.

"Yeah, and why do you suppose our one and only lead didn't make an appearance?"

C.J. failed to suppress a grin. "Because you were laid out on the floor like a gutted fish." He hooted with laughter. "I sure wish you could've seen it. My God, that was a sight!"

At six feet four inches and two hundred and twenty-five pounds, Christian Delacroix wasn't bested by many people. He couldn't believe he'd let his guard down enough for a woman to accomplish the almost impossible. Served him right! That was what he got for letting Mr. Happy do his thinking.

"Yeah. Which is why I'm going to talk to the chief. We need some local help. And I don't care what you think. I'm not going to let that…that woman get away with assault." Not that he was really planning to file charges, but a little chat with the local deputy dog would go a long way toward scaring her. She'd had the temerity to call him "sugar" right before she zapped his butt.

C.J. gave a few more snaps of his gum. "I still think this is a bad idea."

Christian suddenly had the uneasy feeling that C.J. was keeping a secret. He propped his elbows on the table. "Guess what, sport? Objection noted."

"Don't say I didn't warn you."

Christian glared at his friend and continued to prowl the police chief's claustrophobic office. It was the size of a broom closet. He stopped in front of the framed diplomas, the only decoration on the wall. L. L. LaTullipe, B.S., the University of Texas. L. L. LaTullipe, M.A., the University of Houston. Where was the requisite "love me" wall with the plaques and pictures that were de rigueur for any self-respecting police chief?

"Take a look at these. What do you think L.L. stands for?" Christian glanced at C.J., who was grinning like a cat with a saucer of cream. "What's with you?"

"Nothing, not a thing," C.J. replied, but his grin got even broader.

"Hmph!" Christian fell into one of the wooden office chairs and forced himself not to twiddle his thumbs.

Did he have mush for brains? He should be keeping a low profile, not hanging around a cop shop.

"I need a cup of coffee." And he also needed C.J. to stop tapping on the arm of the chair.

"You came on a little strong with the secretary." C.J. continued his rhythmic assault.

"No way was I sitting out in that waiting room. Call and make an appointment—yeah, right. The chief was blowing us off." Christian had used his size and his scowl to gain entrance to the chief's office. It worked every time. No wonder the gate guard hadn't offered them coffee. She was probably checking the mug books for his picture.

Christian was contemplating mug shots himself when he heard a familiar feminine voice out in the hall. It had a lilting Southern accent that was indelibly imprinted on his brain. What was *she* doing at the police station? Stupid question. That woman could create pandemonium by simply walking down the street.

LOLLY FLEW down the hall toward her office. "Dora, you got rid of those guys, didn't you?" she called over her shoulder.

"No, she didn't, *sugar*," a deep baritone voice informed her. "And what are *you* doing here?" He grabbed her upper arms. "They catch you trying to kill some other guy?"

He smelled of sun, detergent and a subtle but distinct—and memorable—aroma. Lolly prayed she was hallucinating, but she couldn't possibly be that fortunate.

It took a few seconds to process that not only were his hands firmly clamped around her arms, but he was also highly irritated. What did *he* have to be mad about? Okay, okay, it was probably the stun gun. But considering the fact that he couldn't keep his hands to himself, he deserved it!

She drew herself up to her full five foot ten and sent him her best steely-eyed cop stare. They didn't call her "boss lady" for nothing.

"Let go of my arms." Her words were so cold they dripped icicles. "And back up. Now!" He complied, but he was gritting his teeth so hard, he was afraid he'd break a molar.

"Need some help, Chief?" Joe stepped forward, his hand on his holster.

Christian's jaw dropped. "Chief?" What did he mean, Chief?

When Joe moved toward him, Christian held both palms in front of his chest. "Hey, man, it's cool. I'm going to reach in my back pocket for my ID." He winced when Joe unsnapped his holster. The way his luck was running, Barney Fife would probably shoot him with his one and only bullet.

"Here." He handed Joe the leather case that held his badge. "I'm Lieutenant Delacroix. One of the good guys." C.J. and Lolly snorted in unison.

Lolly took a deep breath and studied the identification. Unbelievable, the guy was a cop. Not only was he a cop, he was a high-ranking state narcotics cop. Double, double darn!

Since the floor obviously wasn't going to open up and swallow her, it was time to put on her professional act. "I'm Lavinia LaTullipe. But everyone around here just shortens it to Chief. As in *Police Chief.*" She stepped backward and put her hands on her hips. Lolly had no intention of being polite. Just because he was a cop didn't make him one of the good guys.

"Well, *Chief*—" he smirked "—this puts a new complexion on things. I came down here to file charges against some blonde who assaulted me last night. Do you happen to know anything about that?" He took two steps into her personal space.

"Hey, wait a—" Joe started to object, but Lolly put a hand on his arm.

"Joe, would you take C.J. out into the hall and wait? I think this gentleman and I need a little private conversation. I'll just be a minute." Lolly smiled at Joe and waggled a finger at C.J., who was sporting a goofy grin.

Christian frowned at his friend. "Yeah, Cookie, go out in the hall like a good little boy. I'll deal with you later." His threat prompted a chuckle.

Lolly hoped she hadn't made a mistake in sending Joe away. This man had an incredible presence, but she wasn't going to let that unsettle her. No, siree!

Ignoring his glower, she managed to slip behind her desk. "Please, have a seat. I'm sure we can come to some mutually agreeable solution."

"Solution, my rear end. You used a Taser on me." He sat down on the wooden chair. "Gave me a headache I'll have for a week!" He put his elbows on her desk and leaned forward. "So, what are you going to do about this? Arrest yourself?"

He leaned closer, but she was too smart to fall for that particular bullying tactic.

Lolly rolled her chair back and retrieved a notebook from the credenza. "Even in this town, we have procedures." She thumped the binder on the desk. "In the case of inappropriate actions by the police chief, you have redress through the mayor and the city council. All you have to do is walk across the street and talk to the mayor.

I'll call him right now and let him know you're coming over." Lolly picked up the receiver.

Lance was going to have a field day with the fact that she'd stun-gunned a cop. They'd been ribbing each other for the past twenty-nine years, and this would provide fodder for at least another decade.

"Put the phone down." Christian sat back and sighed. "Let's just forget it."

Thank you, God! Lolly couldn't deal with Lance's gloating and two murders at the same time.

"Good." She rose to escort Christian to the door. The sooner he was out of her office, and her life, the better she'd like it. "I have an emergency to take care of."

"What happened, a golf cart heist out at Twisted Oak?" He figured that would get a rise out of her. But instead of commenting, she propped her hip on the desk and stared at him like he was something she should scrape off her shoe.

Gone was the tight-jeans look of last night—replaced by the fashion sense of a spinster schoolteacher. But even the shapeless beige linen jacket couldn't hide her dazzling body, and the scraped-back bun and horn-rimmed glasses didn't disguise her cheekbones and gorgeous cornflower-blue eyes.

"Are you trying to impersonate a prison matron?" Oooh boy, he should talk to a professional about that death wish. But crazy as it was, he wanted to see those eyes flash fire again.

"If you'll excuse me, I have a murder to investigate." She started toward the door.

"Murder? Where? How?"

"Not that it's any of your business, but since you're a cop I'll tell you. A man washed up on the beach."

He rubbed a hand over his eyes. "Not another one." He paused. "I'll bet a million bucks it's Jason Schwartz. He went missing a week ago. Bloody fantastic," he muttered as he stalked around the room. "That's it! My undercover assignment was to investigate these murders, but I think it's time to come out into the open. You need help." He scratched his head in consternation. "I suppose C.J. and I should have contacted you when we arrived."

She skidded to a halt and eyed him. "Yeah, you should have. And what if I don't *want* your help?" She honestly didn't want a buttinski big-city cop second-guessing everything she did. But as much as she hated to admit it, she could use some good forensic assistance. Her small department wasn't equipped to handle crime of this magnitude.

"Too bad. You've got me, anyway. Let's go see what the bad guys have been doing." He took her arm and steered her out of the office.

Chapter Three

Yellow police tape surrounded the area of rock-strewn beach where Peachtree had found the body. Christian and C.J. stood outside the cordoned-off area in order to avoid contaminating the crime scene. Even though the police were taking precautions, it was apparent that the murder had been committed in another location.

C.J. whistled under his breath. "Whoa! What do you think they're feeding the gals around here to grow 'em like that?" He pointed out the dark-haired beauty talking to Lolly. "*That's* one fine-looking woman."

Christian thumped his friend on the arm. "Close your mouth, you're drooling." But who could blame him? The woman was an exotic beauty—tall with waist-length black hair and almond-shaped eyes.

But Christian preferred blondes.

Wait a minute! Where had that come from? And since when did he prefer blondes?

Snap, snap, crackle, pop. When C.J. was deep in thought, his gum popping went into hyperdrive. It drove Christian nuts.

"I don't believe it! That's Olivia Alvarado!" C.J. exclaimed.

"Don't tell me you went to high school with her, too," Christian said. "What were they doing, breeding Miss America candidates?"

"Man, those two weren't *that* gorgeous back then." C.J. waved at Lolly and Olivia. "Believe me, if they were I would've been the first to make a move. But they were both in the honor society." He shook his head ruefully. "They were so smart they scared me."

Christian raised an eyebrow. As far as he knew, nothing scared his partner and friend.

C.J. hadn't taken his eyes off the Hispanic beauty. "I heard Olivia became a vet."

"Get your mind on the job, lover boy, and tell me who that guy is." Christian indicated a man with long gray hair and a beard, wearing white robes. A policeman was taking him over to where Lolly and Olivia stood.

"That's Peachtree," C.J. said. "I heard one of the cops say he found the body."

"What's his story?"

"He's harmless," C.J. laughed. "Been around ever since I was a kid. He lives under the bridge for a while, and then he moves out to the beach. For fun, he stands on the street corner and preaches to the tourists. Can you imagine what he thinks about the thong bikinis?"

Christian snorted and mentally segued to Lolly in a thong. Now, that would stop traffic all the way to Houston! But female curves were the last thing he should be thinking about when he had a murder to investigate.

"WHAT DO you think, Livy?" Lolly asked.

Olivia shrugged and knelt down to examine the body. "I think someone shot our guy with a small caliber gun and then stuck him in a freezer. They let him thaw a bit so he'd float, and then dumped him off a boat." She shook her head. "I'm glad he didn't wash up at the marina. The sight of that—" she waggled her fingers at the corpse "—would set the tourist industry back a decade."

Lolly massaged her temples. "Let me talk this out. We have a perp who has more guts than sense because he obviously dumped the body in broad daylight." She sighed. "A ton of yachts and fishing boats sail this channel everyday. Someone has to have seen *something*." Please, God! Someone saw something.

"Look on the bright side. You won't have a problem identifying him." Olivia picked up the plastic driver's license stapled to the front of the man's shirt. "Even if the ID isn't his, he probably has a record, so his fingerprints will be on file." She fingered the sealed bag of crack rocks tied around his neck.

Lolly squeezed the bridge of her nose. A Tylenol sounded more and more appealing. "Livy, do you have any idea what's happening here?"

Olivia opened her medical bag. "Nope, not a clue. But I'll preserve his hands on the off chance he has some skin under his fingernails." She pulled out her equipment. "I don't think it'll do us any good, because I suspect the killer snuck up on him. Poor jerk probably didn't know what hit him."

She finished her chore and stood up. "We're sending him to the medical examiner in Corpus Christi, aren't we?"

"Yeah." Lolly then spoke to the two attendants who had started to zip the corpse into a black body bag. "I've already called the morgue. They're expecting him."

"Yes, ma'am," one of the men answered as they wheeled the gurney to the ambulance.

"Thank goodness I don't have to cut him open." As the elected coroner, Olivia was responsible for pronouncing the probable cause of death, not conducting autopsies. "A cat or a dog is one thing, but a floater is something else. You know I only took this job to pay off my vet-school loans."

"Lord, Livy." Lolly sighed. "What a mess!"

Before Olivia could respond, one of the men Lolly had sent to search the beach ran up. "Chief. We found two bales of marijuana about a hundred yards up that way." He gestured toward an area where the sand ended and the marshy saw grass took over.

"Hmph." Lolly looked at C.J. and Christian lurking near the police tape. Their body language told her they were dying to get involved. "Guess it's time to call in the big boys—no pun intended." She waved to get Christian's attention.

Swear to goodness, the man was predatory. Couldn't he just walk like an ordinary person? Saunter, skip, stroll—anything would be preferable to that stalking thing he did.

"What can I do to help you, Chief?" He emphasized the last word.

"My men have found some bales of marijuana." She pointed up the beach. "I thought you might be interested."

"I hope I'm not stepping on your toes, but I've already called my captain and he's sending some of our forensics guys. They should be here within the hour. If there's anything here, those guys will find it."

Lolly tried to ignore her irritation at this guy's take-charge attitude.

"My captain wants us to stay around and keep an eye on things," he continued, obviously unaware of her feelings. "C.J.'s going to stay in the field and see what he can learn, but I'll need a desk."

Lolly suppressed the urge to groan in frustration. Now she had to find some place to stuff the big oaf. And the only unoccupied six inches in the whole station house were in *her* office. Oh, yeah—sharing an eight-by-eight space with him sounded like a hoot. Lolly plastered a stiff smile on her face. "I'll see what I can do." Dallas might be far enough away.

She turned to Olivia. "Why don't you come over for dinner tomorrow night?" It was time to get back to the slow and steady pace of her life prior to the advent of dead bodies—and Lieutenant Christian Delacroix.

Chapter Four

Olivia opened Lolly's kitchen door without knocking. "Hey, something smells good."

"I'm making chili." Lolly continued to chop onions. "You want *vino* or sweet tea?"

Olivia took her favorite stool at the kitchen island. "Tea's good. I'm on call this evening. Dr. Bob's up in Houston taking a class on doggy liposuction or some such nonsense. I swear that man can come up with the weirdest things."

Lolly laughed and glanced at her daughter. "Amanda, sweetheart, would you get Miss Olivia some tea? I'm up to my elbows in chili fixin's."

Olivia ruffled Amanda's curls as the child handed her a frosty glass and a bowl of lemons. "How's my favorite kid?"

"Hi, Aunt Livy. You know what? Mama said I could invite some friends to the Ringa Dinga Pizza Palace in Corpus Christi to celebrate the end of school. Then she's going to take us to a movie. Isn't that awesome?"

Olivia's muffled snort got Lolly's attention. "Oh, yeah, that sounds totally awesome."

"Run and do your homework, sweetie," Lolly told her daughter. "Dinner will be ready in about an hour."

Amanda grabbed her books from the kitchen table and skipped off to the living room.

"How many kids are we discussing?" Olivia asked.

"We're up to a dozen." Lolly whacked another onion. "She'd invite her whole class if I let her."

"I know you're a raving lunatic, but you don't have to beat that onion to death."

Lolly took a sip of wine. "Seems to me that you owe me some favors, and I'm calling in my markers. So, Miss Olivia, I think you're going to the Ringa Dinga Pizza Palace with us." She raised an eyebrow to quell any objections.

Olivia leaned back as far as she could and shook her head. "Not me. I've been exposed to Ebola." She giggled. "Would you believe leprosy? Malaria? How about typhoid? I'm sure I'll be in bed at least a month."

"How would you like me to tell Bobby Martin you weren't sick when you cancelled out on that Elks Lodge dance?"

Olivia frowned—and then giggled. "Darn it, Lolly. That's blackmail. Cops aren't supposed to do that kind of thing."

"Probably not. But desperate friends can. So I'm counting you in, right?"

"Oh-kay." Olivia made a choking noise. "When is this little soirée?"

"First weekend in June." Lolly dumped the onions and hamburger into the frying pan. "Unfortunately, that gives me a couple of weeks to dread it, and you a chance to dream up some excuse." She continued to toss in-

gredients into the pot. "I'll be *very* skeptical about anything short of hospitalization."

"Not to change the subject…but I heard through the
grapevine how you stun-gunned that DPS guy, the one
with all the muscles."

The CIA should have a communications system as
accurate as the Port Serenity rumor mill. "Yeah, well."

"Well what?"

"Well, that's not all. I'm also sharing an office with
him."

"And I have to share my office with a thirty-year-old
parrot who screams obscenities. Not fair! We're best
friends and I want the straight skinny."

Lolly sat down and sighed. "Truth—there's something about him that about bowls me over. But there's
no way on God's green earth I'd get mixed up with a
cop, especially after what happened to Daddy."

"That was a long time ago."

"Yes, but Daddy didn't expect to stop the wrong
speeder and get killed. Who *would* expect that? Nope,
this girl's too smart to have anything to do with a narc
cop. That's the absolute worst-case scenario. I want
someone who'll come home every night."

Lolly had barely finished her sentence when her
mother, Marcela Hamilton, aka Mee Maw, strolled in
the back door and unintentionally diffused the gloomy
mood. "It smells good in here." A petite version of Lolly,
she didn't look almost seventy. She'd obviously defied
the aging process. "Aunt Sissy's eating at Luby's Cafe-
teria with her book club, so I thought I'd come over for
supper." Mee Maw was a widow and shared a condo on
the beach with her sister, but every afternoon she stayed
with Amanda until Lolly got home.

Mee Maw hugged Olivia. "Livy, honey, you're gorgeous in that red. I haven't seen you in a month of Sundays. How have you been?"

"I've been fine." Olivia kissed the older woman's cheek. "It's been a while, hasn't it?"

Lolly's mom poured a glass of tea and sat down on one of the bar stools. "I heard something a bit concernin' at bridge yesterday."

A bit concernin' to Mee Maw could be anything from impending Armageddon to an increase in the cost of coffee. But Lolly asked anyway. "What was that?"

"Well, I got this from Prissy Whitaker, and you know how loopy she is, poor thing. She's second cousins with Harvey down at the tire store, and they've had to send him up to that funny hospital in San Antonio a couple of times."

Lolly had a bad feeling about this conversation. When her mother prattled on about second cousins twice removed, it was generally a precursor to *very* unpleasant news.

"Mama!"

"Lavinia Lee LaTullipe, you can just stop giving me that look." Mee Maw shot a glare right back at Lolly.

Darn! She'd never been able to bully the woman.

"Well, anyway. Prissy said Wendell was considerin' coming back to town. Best as I could tell, that band thing he was doing in Houston didn't pan out like he figured it would. At least, that's what Prissy said his mother said." Mee Maw shrugged. "You do remember that Prissy is Mrs. LaTullipe's sister-in-law, don't you?"

Before Lolly could answer, Olivia jumped into the conversation. "Houston? I thought he was in Las Vegas."

"I did, too." Lolly turned to her mother again. "When did he leave Las Vegas? And why is he coming back here?"

Mee Maw shrugged. "Beats me," she said. "But I'll find out. Aunt Sissy has better contacts than the CIA."

Wasn't that the truth! Dear sweet Aunt Sissy had the tenacity of a bulldog and the nose of a bloodhound.

Lolly smacked her forehead. Dead drug dealers, her new office mate, and now Wendell— "I need chocolate. Now!"

Olivia pulled over a stool and hopped up to forage around on the top shelf of the cabinet. "Bingo." She pulled a bag of mini-Snickers out of an electric wok. "New hiding place?"

"Yep, the kids found the other one." Thank goodness the young'uns hadn't discovered the current location of her chocolate courage. "Give me the bag or I'll have to hurt you."

Olivia opened the bag. "And I thought the Ringa Dinga Pizza Palace was going to be bad. Remind me why you married Wendell."

Lolly grabbed a handful of miniature chocolate bars. "He was gorgeous, he was charming and I was very, very young." She shook her head ruefully. "I grew up, and he didn't." That lapse in judgment was the primary reason she was so hesitant to start dating again. There were too many frogs in the dating pool, and she wasn't about to kiss another one. Especially if he was a tall, rugged Texas Department of Public Safety cop—even if she could feel the chemistry all the way to her toes.

Chapter Five

Lolly was exhausted from a long, restless night dreaming about Mr. Rugged, but every Wednesday she had a standing date for breakfast with Olivia at Daisy's Diner. A typical south-Texas greasy spoon, Daisy's specialized in good old-fashioned caffeine, cholesterol and grease. The joint was hopping as usual, but Olivia had managed to snag a booth next to the window.

Lolly waved to indicate she'd seen her friend. Although Lolly didn't hold an elected position, it never hurt to do some back-slapping, baby-kissing and hand-shaking, especially with Mee Maw's buddies. The women were astonishing; if the town needed anything, the blue-haired phenoms found a way to raise the money.

"Is Marcela joining us this morning?" The speaker sported a head of pink helmet hair.

"Yes, ma'am, I'm sure she'll be here shortly," Lolly replied. "You're certainly looking fine this morning, Mrs. Carmichael. Mama says you're doing well since your surgery."

"Sure am. Nice of you to send me that card." Her reply was overwhelmed by raucous laughter from a table where six elderly men, residents of the Twisted

Oak Retirement Village, met every morning to drink coffee and tell war stories.

A masculine voice hailed her from an adjacent table. "Lolly, wait." She'd been so busy talking to Mee Maw's friends she hadn't noticed the two men.

"Hey, Jamison. What's up?" Jamison Thompson was a member of the city council and a royal pain in the patootie. He gave Lolly a hard time on every issue that came before the governing body—from the police budget to the number of tickets written. And he happened to be one of Wendell's old buddies.

"How's business?" Lolly asked, knowing it was a particularly evil question. Everyone in town had heard that Jamison's oil-well-drilling company was on the verge of bankruptcy.

"Not too bad, not too bad."

The man would lie to God, but his friend, Nick, was even worse. Nick, Wendell and Jamison had been buddies since elementary school. Lolly was tempted to ignore the men, but good manners got the best of her. "Hi, Nick."

Nick Abercrombie was one of Corpus Christi's sleaziest criminal defense attorneys. The jerk would do anything to get his clients off. Legal or illegal, it didn't matter.

"Did you know that Wendell's playing with a band in Houston? Vegas didn't work out." Jamison pulled out a chair, but Lolly remained standing.

"Really?" Keep it neutral.

Jamison graced her with an oily smile. "Yeah, really. His band was playing the lounge circuit, but that gig sort of piffled."

"Too bad." The idiots probably didn't realize she was being sarcastic.

"Yeah. I think his new group's going to be playing in a club out on Padre Island. I'll let you know when he gets here."

Lolly smiled. Good, she'd make sure the kids were at camp. Although Wendell rarely used his visitation rights, he created havoc whenever he did.

"I'm having breakfast with Olivia. I've got to run."

"See you around," Jamison said.

Not if she saw him first, he wouldn't.

Olivia was sipping a cup of coffee when Lolly finally made it to the booth.

"What did those two morons have to say?"

Lolly put her head in her hands. "They wanted to let me know Wendell's back in Texas."

"I guess that makes it official."

"I guess so."

Olivia looked over Lolly's shoulder and smiled. "And speaking of trouble, here comes some more."

Before Lolly could ask what her friend meant, she heard a familiar male voice.

"Mind if I sit down with you ladies?"

Christian scooted in next to her. He took up almost all the room on the bench—and she didn't just mean because of his size. It was his whole presence.

The booth was too small and the man was too big. But for some inexplicable reason Lolly didn't consider moving over. The BTUs coming off his thigh could have heated her house for a month, and every time he shifted, his leg rubbed against hers. The man didn't even like her—and there she was, fantasizing about ripping off his clothes and jumping his bones. Did she have no shame?

He signaled for a cup of coffee just as his cell phone

rang. After a few minutes of conversation, he hung up and frowned. "I came over here to tell you I received a fax on the forensics report. No fingerprints, no fibers, nothing. Someone did a good job of cleaning the vic up. Being in the water didn't help."

"We know from the autopsy he was killed with a .25 to the back of the head. Very efficient," Olivia added.

"It doesn't surprise me. That's what they used on the last one." Christian indicated the cell phone on the table. "That call was from Captain Thornton. A drug kingpin out of New Jersey disappeared last night from a nightclub in Houston. A guy named Pavel Romanowski, Russian Mafia, I think. The DEA's been after him for years. Captain wanted to know if we've had any more floaters."

"Oh, God, not another one." Lolly rubbed her face. "If we're lucky, this guy will land in Baytown."

"Yeah, right." Christian snorted, waiting until the waitress filled his cup to continue. "I'm afraid it's the beginning of a drug war."

"Well, we're not going to participate. That nonsense belongs in the big city, not in Port Serenity," Lolly exclaimed.

He stared at her over the rim of his coffee cup. "Don't look now, but it *is* happenin' here." Christian took another sip and set the cup down. "I'll let you know the minute I get any info from Houston. Ladies." He winked before he sauntered off.

"Holy cow!" Olivia fanned her face. "Is that guy as hot as I think he is?"

Lolly watched him. "Yep, I'm afraid so."

Chapter Six

Christian didn't know why he was delivering this report to Lolly on a Saturday—more than likely, it was simple curiosity. He pulled his motorcycle up to the curb and checked out the house. He had to have the wrong address. There wasn't a cop in Texas who could afford a place like that, not unless he was dirty. And that wasn't the Lolly he thought he knew.

He studied the scrap of paper to double-check the address. Sure enough, the 10 Bay View Drive written on the paper matched the number prominently displayed below the Texas Historic Property emblem.

It was a large yellow house built in a typical Gulf Coast style with the main living area elevated to the second-floor level. The twin chimneys, wide front veranda and forest-green storm shutters would have been right at home in Louisiana.

He set the kickstand and dug a manila folder out of the saddlebag.

"Watch out, mister." Christian looked up just in time to spot a football sailing at his head. Reflexes from his college days kicked in as he snatched the ball out of the air and tucked it against his side. He *had* been daydreaming not to notice the teenagers playing "skins and shirts" on the wide front lawn. They reminded him of a bunch of Great Dane puppies, all legs and big feet.

"Great catch." A tall blond kid loped to the fence to retrieve the football. "Have you ever played pro?" he asked as Christian handed him the pigskin.

"I played in college."

"Wow." The kid waved to his cronies. "Hey, everybody! This guy played college football." He reached over the picket fence to shake hands. "I'm Bren."

Wait a minute! It took a minute for Christian to notice that he was leaning on the gate of a *white picket fence!* Damn!

"You want to help us with a couple of plays?" The kid named Bren was obviously the leader of the pack.

Even though it had been quite a while since he'd been on a gridiron, Christian still remembered some things the kids could probably use. "Sure. I can spare a few minutes."

The light finally dawned. Same platinum hair, same blue eyes, same height. Lolly's kid!

"Don't worry about Harvey." Bren indicated a huge black dog. "He'll just try to lick you to death."

Now that was interesting! She had a kid, a dog *and* a picket fence.

THIS HAD BEEN one of the worst weeks of her life, and Lolly was ready for an at-home spa day—bubble bath, hot-oil hair treatment, facial, pedicure, the works.

The boys were playing football on the front lawn, and Amanda and a friend were listening to music in her room. They'd both been warned not to disturb Mom unless they were in imminent danger of death or dismemberment. Broken bones and sprains didn't count.

Lolly uttered a heartfelt sigh. This was the most relaxed she'd felt since all the craziness started. A warm bubble bath, Enya and a locked bathroom door—she was going to stay in the tub until her fingers resembled California raisins.

So far, so good. No "Where is the peanut butter?" or "Can you drive us to the Dairy Queen?"

"Mom, are you still in there?" Oops, spoke too soon!

"Yes, Amanda, I'm still here." Sheesh! Did the kid think she'd shinnied out the bathroom window in her birthday suit?

"When are you getting out?"

"When I get finished."

"Oh...okay."

The natives were restless. It wouldn't be long before Bren and his friends invaded the house.

Lolly donned her ratty bathrobe, wrapped her hair in a towel and slathered a green cucumber beauty mask on her face. It took fifteen minutes for the goop to dry, so that gave her time to paint her toenails. Red Hot Mama was the name of the polish. Lolly figured if she couldn't be a red-hot mama in real life, she could live vicariously through her feet. She stuffed cotton balls between her toes.

"Mother!" Amanda screeched. "Moooother!" the child screamed again.

Lord in heaven! Lolly's maternal instincts whipped into overdrive as she catapulted out of the bathroom and raced down the hall toward the front door. She was a maternal SWAT team in action, a mother bear to the rescue, a towel-wearing, green-faced nincompoop.

Lolly skidded to a stop not two feet from guess who—and he was staring at her like she'd just escaped from an asylum. Why not? She'd made enough racket to wake the dead. Swear to God, if he laughed she was going to deck him.

"Amanda Lavinia LaTullipe! From the way you were screaming, I thought someone was killing you!" Lolly tried to keep her voice calm and rational, but she could hear it going up a note with each syllable. Now she sounded like a raving maniac *and* looked like one. Fantastic!

She pointed down the hall. "To your room."

Lolly whirled to face her visitor. "What can I do for you?"

The man *was* biting his cheek to keep from laughing. The twinkle in his eye gave him away; if he so much as smirked she was definitely going to smack him.

He held up a folder. "I brought some reports that came this morning. I told you I'd pass them on to you as soon as they arrived."

She snatched the folder out of his hand. Fabulous! He was being professional and she was acting like an ill-mannered shrew.

Lolly rubbed her forehead, and in doing so dislodged a large glop of green goo. That was her first mistake. The second was watching the gelatinous mass drop leisurely to the tip of his boot. It was just like watching a car wreck in slow motion.

In unison, they looked down at the offending mess.

There was silence for a few seconds, and then he made a strangling noise—something between a cough and a snort. That did it! If he wanted to laugh at her, he'd have to do it by himself.

She leveled her finger at his chest. "You, go in the living room." Lolly pointed at a door leading off the broad center hall. "It'll take me five minutes to get dressed." And wipe the gunk off her face.

Christian managed to suppress his belly laugh until Lolly was out of earshot. His mama hadn't raised a dummy. Even a chuckle, and he would've been minus a few of his favorite body parts.

THE LIVING ROOM she directed him to was exactly that, a place where people lived. No prissy antiques or collections of breakable porcelain for this family. It was obvious they lived and played right there—Barbie dolls, a couple of baseballs and a basketball, and a bookcase full of paperback novels.

A plump calico cat jumped off the couch and did a perfunctory stretch before she ambled over to a pool of light streaming through the floor-to-ceiling windows to resume her nap.

Christian wandered to the fireplace mantel and picked up one of the framed pictures. The kids were carbon copies of their mother. LaTullipe must have been a poor excuse for a sperm donor. And speaking of Mr. LaTullipe, where was *his* picture? There were pictures of the kids, pictures of two women who appeared to be older versions of Lolly, pictures of Olivia and even a picture of the cat and dog. But there wasn't a single picture of a guy. So where *was* Mr. LaTullipe?

The room was distinctly feminine. Pale yellow walls, furniture upholstered in a muted floral pattern and plants everywhere—not a hint of a grown man in this room. Interesting, very interesting! And she didn't wear a ring….

JUST THE THOUGHT of looking in a mirror sent cold chills down Lolly's spine. She'd resort to a quick shower to get the grease out of her hair and the junk off her face.

Now, if only she could twitch her nose and erase his recent memories, she'd be in business.

Five minutes later, she had her hair jerked up into a ponytail and was searching her closet for a clean pair of jeans. Torn knees would have to do. Ditto for the faded Dallas Cowboys T-shirt.

"I'm sorry it took so long," she said when she joined him. "Have a seat." Lolly waved in the direction of the flowered sofa. "Would you like something to drink? I'm dying for a glass of iced tea." Or a great big shot of Jack Daniel's, straight.

"Sure." He went down the hall with her to the kitchen at the back of the house.

Had the kids loaded the dishwasher? Probably not, the way this day was going.

He nudged a fluffy white cat off the chair and took a seat at the round oak table.

"That's Snowball. She's Amanda's cat," Lolly said.

"Snowball?"

She handed him a glass of tea and sat down. "What can I say? Amanda's never seen snow, so it's probably wishful thinking."

He pointed at the toe she'd managed to paint Red Hot Mama. "Do you always only do one toe?"

Speaking of Red Hot—her face matched her nail enamel. "No. Thanks to Amanda, I was interrupted."

"Hmm." For some reason he kept staring at her toe.

Lolly tapped the manila folder. "I presume these are the forensic reports."

"Yep. Nothing really new. They found a spot of grease on the last guy's clothing. They're working on that. But basically, we're still at square one."

That was what Lolly was afraid of. She was also

afraid the newest missing guy was going to show up on her beach.

"Mama." Amanda stuck her head sheepishly in the kitchen door, her friend close behind. "Can I go to Leslie's house?"

"May I."

"May I go to Leslie's?"

"Sure. But first I need a hug."

A smile lit up the little girl's face as she jumped in her mother's lap. "Smoochy, smoochy."

"Smoochy, smoochy."

The two girls ran out the back door giggling.

Lolly reached for the report, but before she could read it, her office phone rang.

"Oh, great! That's my dispatcher." She grabbed the cordless and clicked it on.

"Chief, I hate to tell you this, but we have another body. They found him in almost the same place as the last."

"Same drill. Call Olivia and tape off the area. I'll be there in a few minutes." She grimaced as she briefed Christian. "I'm afraid the Russian Mafia dude has come calling."

"Put on your shoes. We'll get there faster on my Harley."

Lolly hesitated a moment before she collected her holster and sprinted to the front closet for her boots.

Lolly had her phone in her hand as she followed Christian out to the front porch. "I need to call Leslie's mom." When she hung up, she waved Bren over. "I have an emergency. Amanda's at Leslie's house. Stay home till I get back."

"Aw, Mom."

"Do it."

The teenager looked lovingly at the Harley. "Are you going on *that?*"

Lolly nodded.

"Cool!"

That wasn't exactly her opinion. She stared at the huge black motorcycle with its chrome shining in the sun and suppressed a shudder. Lord help her!

Christian gave her the extra helmet and adjusted her chinstrap. "Hop on."

She tentatively put her hand on the seat. "Yeeew."

He made clucking noises as he straddled the seat.

That did it! Lolly mounted the bike.

"You'll love it."

Highly unlikely.

"Put your arms around my waist."

Not in this lifetime! She'd be fine hanging on to the seat. He chuckled just before he gunned the engine. Big mistake! It took a nanosecond to realize she wasn't going to be able to stay on the blasted thing. Lolly squealed and hung on to his waist for dear life.

Jiminy Christmas! The way she was plastered to his back from chin to crotch, she felt every inch of him, heard every breath he took. Whoa!

THIS CAME AS CLOSE to purgatory as he wanted to get, and it was all his fault. When had he turned into a masochist? He needed to rearrange the erection that had sprung to life the moment she pressed her breasts against his back. Crap, she didn't act as if she even liked him. So why did he have a terminal case of the hots? Even with the gunk on her face, she was adorable. And her mind wasn't bad, either. But business came first—romance or lust or whatever it was had to go on the back burner.

Christian pulled his bike into an abandoned industrial complex. The rusted sign on the front gate indicated that the place was originally a packinghouse. Now it was just a cluster of boarded-up buildings. Cruisers were parked next to the dock, and some uniformed officers stood outside the yellow police tape.

Lolly had removed her helmet and jumped off the bike almost before Christian secured the kickstand.

"I called C.J. before we left your house. I told him to meet us here. And speak of the devil," Christian said as he watched C.J. park his Jeep.

His partner hopped out of the car and sauntered over. "Another floater?"

"Yeah," Lolly answered as she joined the men.

She knelt to examine the corpse. "We've been expecting you." Lolly snapped on a pair of latex gloves and gingerly picked up a soggy New Jersey driver's license.

"Romanowski?" Christian asked.

She drew off the latex gloves. "Yep. Have you called your lab guys?"

"Yeah. I'm beginning to think we need to station one of 'em up here." Christian scrubbed his face. "The mileage is killing my budget. Not to mention the overtime."

"Yep, I know what you mean," Lolly concurred.

C.J. grinned and pointed at Olivia, who was across the sandy parking lot.

"Chief, there's your buddy. The doctor-coroner lady."

Olivia ducked under the police tape. "Hey, Lol. Why don't these guys pick Galveston to go swimming?" She opened her bag and took out a pair of gloves to roll the body over and study the entrance wound in the back of his head. "Obviously we can't tell the caliber, but it's similar to the other victims. Who found this one?"

Sergeant Joe answered. "It was Peachtree again. He's over there." The man in question was sitting under a twisted live oak tree.

Christian was halfway to the witness before Lolly caught up with him. "Do you think he knows anything?" she asked.

"Nope. But I'm curious about this Peachtree guy." Christian walked up to the witness.

"Sir." Christian extended his hand. "I'm Lieutenant Delacroix with the Texas Department of Public Safety, Narcotics Services." He reached into his back pocket for his badge. "We need to ask you a few questions."

"Certainly. I'm more than glad to help." Peachtree frowned. "This used to be a peaceful place to live. But it's not anymore. I'm thinking of moving across the channel."

"Did you see anything before you found the body?" Lolly asked.

He stroked his beard before he answered. "No, ma'am, Miss Lolly. Least not today. Last night when I was scavenging for driftwood, I saw a boat out there a couple of hundred yards."

Christian's ears perked up. "What kind of boat?"

"It was too far away to see anything but its running lights. It was big." This witness might not be as helpful as Christian had hoped.

"Big like a yacht or big like a barge?" he asked.

"Could've been a yacht or it could've been a fishing boat. It wasn't a tugboat because it didn't sound powerful enough."

"Thanks, Peachtree." Lolly joined the conversation. "Sergeant Joe will drive you down to the station to take your statement. If you remember anything else, please call me."

"Yes, ma'am. I'll surely do that."

While Christian and Lolly questioned Peachtree, C.J. went to speak to Olivia. "Do you suppose they'll get anything from him?" He grinned at her.

"I doubt it." Olivia only vaguely remembered C.J. from high school, and what she remembered wasn't all that wonderful. Boy, had he changed! Now he had a killer smile that he used frequently. And with his sun-bleached hair, sea-foam-green eyes and cocky little-boy grin, the guy was absolutely gorgeous. No doubt about it—he had flirting down to a fine art and for some crazy reason he was focusing all that charm on her.

"Say, Doc. What made you decide to be a vet?"

From anyone else, it would have been an innocuous question. But coming from him it rankled.

Olivia put on a saccharine smile. "Because I like dogs better than most of the guys I've met."

"Ouch!" He clutched his heart. "You're a hard, hard woman. You know that?"

To her surprise, he leaned down and whispered in her ear. "But this time you've met your match, sweetheart."

Before she could come up with a suitable retort, the irritating man took off to talk to a couple of the uniforms.

Two hours later, it was a wrap. The crime scene was secure, the body and Peachtree were routed to their respective destinations and the lab boys were scouring the area.

Christian joined Lolly and Olivia. "Let's get a bite to eat. I'm starved."

"Me, too. But first I need to call home," Lolly said.

Olivia twisted her hair into a scrunchie. "I'm on. Dr. Bob's got everything under control at the clinic."

Christian motioned his friend over. "Hey, C.J., you want to go to Becker's for barbecue?"

C.J. WINKED at Olivia. He'd known many beautiful women, but there was something special about the gorgeous vet. This Port Serenity gig was pretty danged interesting, after all. Dead bodies, a Latin lovely with an attitude—and what was going on between the boss and the chief?

Yep, this was turning into a mighty entertainin' assignment!

Chapter Seven

Becker's BBQ had a familiar smell of mesquite wood smoke and the rustic atmosphere of an old-time dance hall. Diners could order takeout or enjoy their food at wooden picnic tables spread throughout a cavernous room that in a previous life had been a barn. Neon beer signs beckoned the patrons to try Coors, Shiner Bock and Lone Star. Waitresses were nonexistent.

Tony Becker, an old high school friend, manned a counter featuring beef brisket, ribs, coleslaw, beans and potato salad. "Hey, Chief, what's up?"

"Hi, Tony. I'll take the brisket plate and a peach cobbler."

Christian was behind her in line. "I'll have the brisket, double the meat, an extra side order of coleslaw and beans, apple pie and a Budweiser." He gave the steaming plate of barbecue an appreciative glance. "You might not have noticed, but I'm a growing boy."

Lolly knew all about feeding a growing boy.

Since it was Saturday, the place was crowded, but Lolly spotted a table in the far corner. Typical of a small town, a number of people greeted Lolly and Olivia as they made their way to the back of the restaurant.

When she sat down, Christian plopped on the bench beside her. Great! She was going to have to eat elbow-to-elbow with him. Olivia didn't look any happier with the situation; C.J., however, was sporting an enormous grin.

"Mmm." Lolly dove into her meal. "I didn't know how hungry I was."

During a lull in the munching, Christian took his napkin and dabbed at her chin. "You have sauce on your face."

Great, now she was *wearing* part of her meal. What next—a big zit on the end of her nose?

"You have a wonderful house," Christian commented.

That one came out of left field. "Thanks. It's been in our family for over a hundred and fifty years." Lolly smiled proudly. "It even has a name—Hamilton House. Pretty cool, huh?"

"Pretty cool," Christian agreed. He'd never known anyone who lived in a house with a name.

"My mama gave it to us when I was pregnant with Bren. It's tricky sometimes because she walks in like it's still her place. But hey, we make it work."

"I hate to be nosy. But where is Mr. LaTullipe?"

"Wendell's dad lives in Corpus Christi most of the year, but they might be at their place in Guadalajara right now." Lolly addressed Olivia. "Livy, do you know?"

Before Olivia could answer, Christian tried again. "I mean your husband."

"My husband? You mean Wendell?" Lolly and Olivia shared a laugh. "My ex-husband left a long time ago."

"And good riddance," Olivia muttered.

"Wendell succumbed to star-itis shortly after Amanda was born. He went to Las Vegas with his band buddies. He decided he was going to find fame and fortune but—" she laughed "—I don't think it worked out."

"Oh." There wasn't a whole lot Christian could say. Against all the odds, he was incredibly attracted to her. And if he wasn't completely delusional, the feeling was mutual.

"He has visitation rights, but he rarely uses them. Fatherhood is not Wendell's long suit."

"That's too bad," Christian said.

"No, it's not." Olivia put in her two cents' worth. "Wendell's a nitwit. Always has been."

"Now, Livy, he has some good points."

"Name 'em."

"He's kind to his mother and he makes great kids."

"Okay, I'll give him those, but not anything else," Olivia conceded, then changed the subject. "If you want to hear something funny, ask her about her name."

"Okay, I'll bite. What about your name?"

Lolly frowned at her friend but continued. "Remember I told you we've had Hamilton House in our family since before the Civil War? The ancestor who built the house was a blockade runner for the Confederacy and his wife was named Lavinia." She grimaced. "I know this sounds nuts, but every generation since has named a girl Lavinia. Thus, we have Lavinia Lee, that's me, and Amanda Lavinia, my daughter."

"How about your mother?" C.J. asked.

"Nope, in that generation it was Aunt Sissy's turn. Her name is Lavinia Louise. And, *Cookie* Baker, don't you dare snicker. Your family's just as nuts as mine."

They were all laughing about crazy Southerners when Lolly's cell phone chirped. Oh, no! She could do without any more bad news today, thank you. But when she heard Cletus's voice she knew she was out of luck. Her deputy didn't call just to chitchat.

"What do you need?" she asked.

When he hesitated, her heart sank.

He finally answered. "I have Bren and a couple of his buddies in the back of my car."

It was a certain fact he wasn't taking the kids out for a spin. "What's he done?"

"They were spray-painting graffiti on the beach signs," Cletus answered. "What do you want me to do with them?"

"Bring them to my office. I'll be there in ten minutes." She was going to throttle her firstborn.

"Anything wrong?" Olivia asked.

Lolly did a quick replay and asked her friend for a ride to the police station.

Olivia included the guys in the conversation. "My dad's the park supervisor, so they'll probably call him, too. If anyone can put the fear of God into those kids, it's Raoul Alvarado."

THE TENSION IN THE KITCHEN was as thick as the syrup Lolly was pouring on her pancakes. And thanks to the efficient rumor mill, Mee Maw had made it to the house before the sun came up.

Lolly took a deep breath. She didn't intend to make any more of this than necessary. "Bren, I hope you understand you got off easy this time."

"Mom," he whined, but stopped when she raised an eyebrow.

"Young man, just thank your lucky stars that Mr. Alvarado agreed to let you guys clean his beach all summer. Believe me, I would've come up with a much more painful way for you to pay off the cost of those signs."

The kid knew when he was beat. "Yes, ma'am."

"And you're also grounded for the next week. School, baseball practice, home. No calls, no visiting friends, nothing."

"Mommm." Again he stopped in midwhine. "May I be excused to go start my prison sentence?"

Lolly wanted to smack him, but nodded.

"Amanda, if you're finished with breakfast, why don't you call Leslie."

Amanda obviously wanted to catch all the gossip, but she reluctantly obeyed.

When Lolly was sure Amanda was out of earshot, she turned to her mother. "Okay, spill it. You've been dying to say something ever since you came in the door."

Mee Maw threw back her head and laughed. "Do you remember the time you and Olivia threw bottles of tempera paint at the school building during eighth-grade graduation?"

Lolly winced. She wasn't likely to forget that event.

"I remember a couple of young ladies who scrubbed that wall for two weeks."

"Yeah, but you weren't the police chief. It's different."

"I understand. Preachers' kids, principals' kids and police chiefs' kids, they all have a hard row to hoe."

"I know." In this case, her mom was right. "All in all, what they did wasn't that bad." She sighed loudly. "He needs a father." Just as soon as things got back to a dull roar, Lolly intended to find a nice, steady, responsible man.

"That'll be a little difficult. You haven't had a date since the Stone Age."

"Mother, don't!"

"Well, it's true. What about this Christian fellow? Lately his name crops up in every sentence you utter."

"Mom! He's a cop!"

"So are you. So what?"

"He chases drug dealers. He deals with the slimiest of the slimy. I will not—I *cannot*—get involved with a narc cop. Do you have *any* idea what they do?" This was not a conversation she wanted to have with her mother.

Mee Maw lifted Lolly's chin. "Does this have anything to do with your daddy?"

Ouch! She was getting too close to the truth for comfort. And much as Lolly wanted to deny it, the truth was obvious.

"Oh, honey." Mee Maw dabbed at the tears running down her daughter's face. "Your daddy would want you to be happy, and sometimes being happy means taking a chance. There aren't any guarantees in life."

Lolly sniffed and wiped her eyes.

"And, let me tell you, if I was thirty years younger I'd hog-tie that man myself. Whew! That one's hot!"

Chapter Eight

Christian's trip to Houston had been an exercise in futility. His informant was long gone, and who could blame him. The place resembled a shooting gallery.

Someone was responsible for the war—and that someone had an agenda. But what was it? Unfortunately, all the people willing to talk had nothing to tell him.

It was almost eight o'clock before he drove into Port Serenity. He needed a shower, a good meal and a soft bed, but more than anything he wanted to see Lolly. The lot behind the station was almost empty, but her Blazer was still in her reserved slot. Christian desperately wanted to talk to someone who didn't begin and end every sentence with the word *mother*. And unfortunately, those dudes weren't invoking a maternal figure.

Christian turned off the truck engine and rubbed his neck. One look at her Blazer, and he was back in fantasyland. He could close his eyes and imagine the scenario. He'd walk in and Lolly would be wearing a smile and the flowery perfume that always made him think of spring. Then she'd look up and tell him she'd been waiting.

Sure, and the moon was made of blue cheese. But the great thing about a fantasy was that he could have it any way he wanted it. And undoubtedly he wanted Lolly, even if he wasn't any good for her.

The light at the end of the hall lured him like a beacon. Christian leaned against the door and watched her tap on the keyboard. Now, if only he could conjure up a brilliant one-liner that would drive her into his arms. Instead, the lamest comment in the world came out of his mouth. "What are you doing here so late?" Smooth move, Ex-Lax! He sounded like a pimple-faced computer nerd.

Her hands flew to her chest. "Heavens, didn't anyone ever tell you not to sneak up on a woman carrying a gun?"

That comment elicited a chuckle. "No. Can't say I've heard that one before."

Swear to goodness, the man was just too sexy and the way he wore a pair of jeans—oooh, boy! "Well, people have been killed for less. And why are *you* here so late?"

Christian lounged on the corner of her desk. "I just got back from Houston and saw your car in the parking lot."

Her stomach growled. "Oh, my word." She slapped a hand across her stomach. "It's been crazy around here and now my tummy's talkin' to me."

He reached for her hand. "I'm starved. Let's go to the Surf and Turf for dinner. My treat. You can tell me about your day."

She was starving. But the Surf and Turf? Forget it! "I'm not dressed for anything fancy." Not to mention that the place was way too romantic, at least when it came to Mr. Sexy and those pesky pheromones of hers. "How about Taco Bell?"

"Nope. I'm dying for a steak and a huge baked potato." He tossed his keys at her. "And you can drive. I'm pooped."

His truck was just like the man—big, tough and impossible to maneuver. "Don't talk to me until I get this thing out of the parking lot," she instructed. It felt like she was handling a Greyhound bus. When she finally managed to get out on the street, she took a deep breath. "What did you find out in Houston?"

"Nothing that we didn't already know. We have a drug war going on, and Pavel's untimely demise was the latest volley." He leaned his head against the leather seat. "Please tell me another corpse didn't wash up on the beach today."

"Nope. Lots of other stuff, but no bodies." She paused as she thought back over her day. "We had a suspicious fire at the RV park. Probable arson."

"What makes you think it was arson?"

"My great deductive reasoning, and the fact that we found a gas can. The disgruntled girlfriend of the guy who owns the trailer works at an Exxon station. Guess where the can came from. Duh! She confessed when Joe went out to talk to her. End of case. Now, back to Houston. I want details."

"A couple more guys have fallen off the radar screen," Christian said with a sigh. "We don't know if they left voluntarily or not. Sometimes when it gets hot, they just take off. That's why I asked about new bodies."

"So what do you think?"

"I think we'd better be prepared. This is far from over. All my guys have called in their chits, and we haven't discovered anything useful." He rubbed his chin. "A motive would help."

Lolly frowned thoughtfully. "Let's play *what if.* What if we have a group of do-gooders? Sort of like the Guardian Angels, Gulf Coast version. And they're getting rid of the drug dealers to make the streets safer."

Christian snorted and shook his head. "Dream on. This isn't Sherwood Forest. It's about money. Big money."

"Yeah," she said after a moment. "You're probably right." But why Port Serenity? They had a big seasonal population of Houstonites who owned vacation villas in Pelican Cay, but surely those folks wouldn't be involved in the drug trade.

Lolly and Christian lapsed into companionable silence, contemplating drug wars and motives, until they arrived at the restaurant. In a town of tearooms and shrimp shacks, the Surf and Turf, with its white tablecloths and expensive menu, was a rose in a field of sunflowers. Lolly couldn't remember the last time she'd been here. Lately, a trip to the Tastee Freeze was a treat, and a meal in a place like this was going to be a delight.

It was just as she remembered—soft lighting, linen tablecloths and prices that exceeded her food budget for a week. But hey, he'd volunteered to buy, and how could a girl refuse? She planned to have something scrumptious and fattening. Fish that didn't come in a stick form sounded tempting.

An hour later, Lolly pleated her linen napkin as she studied her dinner companion. The man had just polished off a gigantic steak and now he was studying the dessert menu. The hunk of beef he ate could have fed a family of four.

"That hit the spot." He looked at her empty plate. "Looks like you enjoyed yours."

Lolly suspected her redfish fillets had been good, but she hadn't really tasted anything. It felt like she was on a *date*, and she *wasn't* ready for a date, not with Mr. Sexy.

He leaned back and smiled. "Do you come here

often?" Apparently he'd decided he was going to have to carry the conversational ball.

What had happened to her social skills? "No. Actually this place is out of my league, both kid wise and money wise. We're more of a Shrimp Shack kind of family."

"That's the restaurant down by the marina, right?"

"Yeah, for $5.99 you can get shrimp and fries, chicken and fries or steak fingers and fries. Everything's guaranteed to clog your arteries. Picnic tables and grease. My kids love it."

"I'll have to try it sometime. Red meat, grease—doesn't get much better. Do you want dessert?"

No, she wanted him. Not that he was sweet, but in his black T-shirt and tight jeans he was dangerous and delectable. Someone should just go ahead and plaster *U.S. Prime* right on his rear. She surreptitiously checked out the rest of the clientele. He and the Docksider-wearing yuppies were definitely from different planets.

He waved his fingers in front of her face. "Earth to Lolly. Dessert?"

"Sure." Bring it on. She could use a megadose of endorphins. "Make it something gooey and chocolate."

HE COULD TELL she was nervous—and she should be. If she had even an inkling of what he was thinking she'd hotfoot it out of the restaurant. She'd played with her napkin, the silverware and her wineglass. Now she was twirling chocolate fudge sauce around with her spoon. Oh, man, the things he could do with that chocolate sauce.

Christian picked up an almost-empty bottle. "More wine?"

"Hmm. Yes, I think so." She giggled and held up her glass for a refill.

Next, he indicated her dessert plate. "Are you finished?"

"Hmm. Yes."

Christian signaled their waiter. "Let's go walk on the beach. I need some exercise." That wasn't all he needed but it was all he'd get....

MILES OF ESTUARIES and a rocky coast dotted with sandy beaches and thickets of live oaks growing up to the water's edge provided a haven for the exotic birds and sea creatures of the Texas Gulf Coast. In the winter, Port Serenity was a bird haven; in the summer it was Xanadu for art lovers and wine connoisseurs. Located on the Inter-Coastal Waterway, the city was protected from the rough-and-tumble waves of the Gulf of Mexico.

Christian glanced at the woman strolling down the beach beside him. If he lived to be a hundred, he'd never understand the female mind. Finesse and charm were fairly foreign concepts to him, and never in a million years would he get in touch with his inner child, or his feminine side. Shoot—if he had a feminine side, he'd probably make a pass at it.

He couldn't think of Lolly without remembering her picket fence, shaggy dog and blond kids. That was when he wasn't fantasizing about revealing her luscious flesh, inch by luxurious inch.

Oh, man! He had to get a grip. Not only was she a colleague, she was a forever-after, toothbrush-sharing girl. And until he got his life in order, Christian wasn't ready to form any kind of permanent relationship. At least, that was what he kept telling himself.

"The kids are doing a good job cleaning up the beach." She made the comment as they passed a sign the boys had defaced.

"That was a fitting punishment for them. I imagine this place gets pretty nasty after a holiday weekend."

"No kidding. I told Bren to wear rubber gloves, but I'll bet you money he doesn't. Not macho enough."

Lolly removed her sandals to walk through the gentle waves lapping on the shore. "Why don't you take off your shoes? The sand feels good squishing between your toes."

Christian shook his head. "No way. That's not macho enough." He laughed and looked down at his boots. "You'd never find Segal or Stallone squishing sand between their toes."

They walked past the marina to the end of the public beach. The early-evening walkers had adjourned to dinner, leaving them alone to enjoy the light ocean breeze.

Lolly wandered onto a fishing dock and sat down. Christian was right behind her. "I love it when the wind isn't blowing hard enough to knock you over," she said. Strong ocean winds were the norm. The bent and gnarled live oak trees, a distinguishing feature of the area, were a testament to the force of nature.

It wouldn't take much to reach over and stroke the side of her smooth cheek. But before Christian could act on that impulse she continued the conversation.

"What made you decide to be a narc cop?"

Leave it to Lolly to get to the heart of the matter. That was an excellent question, even if it wasn't any of her business. But if he kissed her—and he was going to kiss her—it probably would be her business. Oh, yeah, it would definitely be her business.

"The first answer that comes to mind is that I want to be one of the good guys. And," he added with a shrug, "I had an older brother who died of an overdose."

She instinctively took his hand. "I'm so sorry."

"Yeah, well, it was a long time ago. He'd been running with a rough crowd, but I think he was about to get it together. He had a football scholarship to Tulane. The night of graduation, he overdosed on heroin and it killed him."

She remained silent as she rubbed the back of his hand.

"The guy he got the stuff from was a local punk." He looked off across the water. "From the time I was in the academy, I wanted to be a narcotics cop. If I can keep one kid alive, I've fulfilled my goal."

"How did your parents cope with losing a child?" Lolly couldn't imagine losing Bren or Amanda.

Christian ran his hand down his face. "They coped, but I don't think my mom's ever really gotten over it. I guess that's why I've always felt I had a mission—but I have to admit I'm tired of it. Sometimes I feel like I'm drowning in all the sleaze." He shifted on the bench, angling his upper body toward her.

"Enough of that." He tucked a curl behind her ear. "What do you want to be when you grow up?"

Lolly smiled contentedly. "I'm very happy just as I am. I love my job. I have a great family. The kids drive me nuts sometimes, but that's in their job description." The man could give Lucifer lessons in dark and dangerous. Not to mention those eyes, which were exactly the color of Hershey's syrup. And the eyelashes... What was a man doing with eyelashes like that? Hey, if she could keep babbling long enough, maybe he wouldn't kiss her, because if he did, she was toast.

She was close enough to see the flecks of gold in his eyes and hear the hitch in his breathing. At least this was affecting him as much as it was affecting her. Lolly's mind told her kissing him would be a terrible mistake, but her body had a different opinion. That rebellious creature was demanding it, clamoring for it. Lolly tilted her chin and opened her mouth just as he put his lips to hers.

At first their kiss was soft and sensual, but like a match scraped slow-motion across sandpaper, the sparks ignited a wildfire of passion, of lust—heavens above, she didn't know *what* it was, but it was hot!

He threaded his fingers through her hair and held her as if he thought she was going somewhere. No way! She'd never been kissed like this before. It was better than the Fourth of July fireworks. It was a banana split, size-eight bathing suit, first-kiss kind of wonderful!

Lolly ran her hands up under his T-shirt. She loved the crisp feel of the hair on his chest and the way he tensed when she rubbed her palms across his nipples.

He pushed her blazer off her shoulders and drew his fingers up her rib cage to play with the underside of her breast.

"You're killing me!" He rested his forehead against hers.

The feeling was mutual.

"We're on a public pier. What do you think the mayor would say if we got arrested for indecent behavior?" he whispered.

Oh, my word! She was so out of control she would've let him have his way with her right in front of God and the entire populace of Port Serenity.

"I guess I got carried away." Her face was no doubt fire-engine red.

He kissed her quickly. "Me, too. That was pretty awesome." He pulled her to her feet. "But I think I'd better get you home."

And then he'd go back to his own place and into an ice-cold shower. Oh, boy—did he ever need to get his head on straight!

Chapter Nine

Sheesh! This was unbelievable. If murder and mayhem weren't enough, she'd had to attend the autopsy on their latest victim. If she lived to be a hundred, Lolly would never get used to autopsies—not the smell, or the clinical detachment, or even worse, the macabre humor.

Then there was the matter of Christian and *the kiss*. Swear to goodness, she should've given him a desk in the men's room. What in the world had possessed her to presume she could share an office with that man? It was like sharing a tree with a panther. By the time five o'clock rolled around, she was exhausted.

In a normal year, and this was turning out to be anything but, May was Lolly's favorite month. Flowers were in bloom, the summer heat hadn't set in, and there was always a festival or a cookout. It was also the lull between when the snowbirds took their RVs back to Wisconsin and the bikini-wearing sun worshippers arrived. In spring and early autumn, the natives could reclaim their town. This May, however, murder had pushed everything else aside.

Lolly was distracted as she drove up the shell-covered drive and parked behind her house. Her day bright-

ened when Amanda and her friend Leslie ran down the
back steps full of giggles and little-girl nonsense.

"Hey, Mom, Leslie and I are gonna ride our bikes
over to her house to put on some Britney Spears
makeup. Is that okay?"

A trip to Leslie's house definitely fell into the okay
category; she wasn't so sure about the Britney Spears
stuff. Jeez Louise. When had her baby stopped playing
with dolls and started smearing on mascara?

"Okay. But be home by six for supper." Lolly was already beginning to miss the big sloppy kisses. "How
about some sugar for your mom?" Lolly put her cheek
down to kid level.

Amanda giggled, but puckered up and obliged. "Mee
Maw has a boyfriend with her." Both of the girls broke
into peals of laughter.

"What do you mean, she has a boyfriend?" Mee Maw
hadn't had a male companion in almost fifteen years.
She was probably entertaining one of her friends from
the senior center.

"Oh, Mrs. LaTullipe." Leslie was giggling so hard she
could barely tell her story. "Mee Maw and this guy were
sitting on the couch kissing and holding hands. Then this
other guy came over and now they're playing poker."

Great, just what Lolly needed—a ménage à trois!
After squealing on the seniors, the girls skipped off and
Lolly opened the kitchen door.

"Mother, I'm home." She locked her holster in the
rolltop desk. If her little spies were right, the shenani-
gans were taking place in the front part of the house.
She'd better let them know an adult was around.

"We're in the dining room. Get a drink and come join
us." That was Aunt Sissy's voice.

Lolly poured a big glass of iced tea. What she wouldn't give for a margarita...

"Aunt Sissy, I didn't know you were coming over." Lolly hugged her aunt. The dining room table was littered with cards and nickels, and right in the middle sat a pair of pink pumps. "Amanda said you guys were playing poker."

Aunt Sissy had the grace to blush. "We started playing five-card stud, but when the girls left, I suggested strip poker." She lifted her bare feet. "I lost the first hand."

Lolly resisted the urge to run, not walk, to the liquor cabinet. Was everyone crazy? Just the thought of her mother in nothing but a bra and panties was enough to make Lolly break out in a cold sweat.

"Mother." Lolly rolled her eyes. "What if Bren came home early from baseball practice?"

Mee Maw smiled broadly. "Don't worry. Bren called and said the coach wants the team to stay for an extra-long practice."

The two men looked sheepish as they stood and waited to be introduced. Her mother was wearing a huge grin. No doubt about it—they'd been playing patty-cake. Question was, which lucky fellow got Mee Maw and which one was stuck with Aunt Sissy? Her aunt was a lovely lady, but she was nuttier than a fruit-cake.

"Bill, this is my daughter, Lolly." Mee Maw patted the man's hand.

The object of her mother's affection was a tall, handsome man in his midseventies with pewter-gray hair and glasses. Carl, his friend, was about the same age, but he was as portly as Bill was thin.

"Bill moved here two years ago. He owns a well-drilling company. His son's running it for him now. And during Vietnam he was in the CIA. Imagine that, I know a real live spy." Mee Maw giggled. "Carl's a retired crop duster. I met him at Piggly Wiggly about five years ago. Did I tell you he flew for Air America back in the 60s? That was the CIA airline, you know."

Lolly studied the alleged pilot. At this point they'd have to use a shoehorn to get him into a cockpit. And the CIA connection sounded like a stretch, too.

"Bill, Carl and some of their buddies are in the Wednesday Night Poker Club." Terrific—her mother had anted up her skivvies to a bunch of card sharks. "Six of the guys from the retirement community at Twisted Oaks play poker every Wednesday night, and twice a year they go to Las Vegas to gamble. Now they want to help the town by forming a citizens' traffic brigade. I told them you'd be thrilled."

Wait a minute! What did her mother just say?

Lolly put on her best cop glare. "Rewind that last sentence. What did you just say?"

"I told them you'd give them some lessons on using the radar gun. With all these murders, your force is running thin. They can assist with traffic control." Mee Maw smiled at Bill. The object of her affections returned the grin.

Oh, boy! A bunch of septuagenarian deputy dogs with radar guns.

"Mother! Would you join me in the kitchen?" It would take great restraint, but Lolly was going to resist the urge to stomp away and bang some pots and pans.

"Miss Lolly. If this is a problem, just let us know. We're only trying to help. Senior citizens are invisible to most people. That's why we make great spies, and even better policemen. Plus, some of us have stuff from our younger years that we'd like to make up for, and what better way than to help the police?" Bill had a big smile on his face. "But we surely don't want to cause any trouble between you and your lovely mother." He patted Mee Maw's hand.

Lolly could understand why her mother was smitten; the man was a charmer. She huffed out a breath and rubbed her temples. "Okay. I'll get Joe to give you a class, and then we can do a test run. You won't have any police powers, but we'll put you where we have the worst problem with speeders. You can record the speed and the car ID. They won't get a ticket, but we can send them a letter. Sometimes that helps."

Mee Maw grinned from ear to ear. "Oh, Lolly, that's wonderful. See, I told you she'd love your idea."

Not exactly accurate—but, what the hey! "Call Sergeant Joe and make an appointment. I'll fill him in on what we're doing."

Her department was stretched to the breaking point, and maybe Mee Maw's friends *would* be a help. With Sergeant Joe training them, they'd probably do fine. At least a girl could hope.

Things were hectic and confusing, but without the murders she wouldn't have had Christian hanging around. Unfortunately, she couldn't decide if that was a blessing or a curse.

Chapter Ten

Two days later, Lolly was up to her eyeballs in paperwork. The preliminary budget was due next month and she was supposed to deliver the department's annual report at the next council meeting. The murder investigations had depleted her slush fund, so she'd have to ask the council for an emergency appropriation. They'd probably have a fit—especially Wendell's old buddy, Jamison.

"Chief." Sergeant Joe tapped on the open door. "We have an incident on Main Street you probably want to know about." It looked suspiciously like he was suppressing a laugh.

"What now?" she snapped and threw down her pen. Then she sighed. "Sorry. I've had a rough morning. What's going on?"

"You remember the guys from the retirement community that I taught to use the radar gun?"

How could she forget them? "Yes."

"They're in the middle of an altercation. Mrs. Pomerantz is mixed up in it, too. Oh," he added, grinning, "your mother's there."

"Nooooo!"

"Yup. I'll hold down the fort while you go check it out." He chuckled all the way down the hall.

She didn't have time for this, but if it involved her mother, Mrs. Pomerantz and the deputy dogs, she'd make the time.

Mrs. Pomerantz and her '65 Chevy Impala were town fixtures. Lolly didn't really need to know if the little old lady still had a driver's license. She was barely as big as a minute, and she could only see out of her land yacht through the hole in the steering wheel. If you happened to be sitting behind her at a light, you'd swear there wasn't anyone driving. Everyone in town knew to get out of her way.

Lolly couldn't remember *ever* seeing a traffic jam on Main Street, but that was exactly what she encountered. Not only was there a traffic jam, most of the cars had been deserted while their occupants watched the action.

She could see the lights from Cletus's patrol car. Thank goodness there was at least one adult on the scene.

"Doesn't anyone work in this town," Lolly muttered as she pushed through the crowd.

"Hey, Chief, this is better than a parade." Mayor Lance Barton put his arm around her shoulder. "Maybe we should make it an annual event. Kind of like celebrity boxing."

She scowled. "Did anyone ever tell you that you have a weird sense of humor?" She plucked his arm off her shoulder. "You're the politician—help me get this under control."

The "this" she was referring to was a knock-down, drag-out fight with Mee Maw as one of the primary combatants. Her mother wound up and whacked a burly tourist with her purse. The guy had on black dress shoes, white kneesocks and plaid Bermuda shorts—maybe he deserved to be whacked.

"Mother! Drop that thing." First it was Bren and his Picasso act, and now her mother was playing Mike Tyson.

Lolly made a quick assessment of the situation. The Impala was in the middle of the street with the driver's door open, Mrs. Pomerantz and Mee Maw were duking it out with the tourist and the deputy dogs were cheering. Mrs. Pomerantz had a right cross? Who'd a thunk it!

"Quiet!" Lolly used her best cheerleader voice.

"You!" She pointed at Bill. "Put the radar gun down. And all of you listen up."

The combatants stopped fighting but continued to scowl at each other.

"Over on the sidewalk," she ordered.

Wonder of wonders—everyone moved in the right direction. "Cletus, would you get the Chevy to the side of the street, please?"

"Yes, ma'am. Be happy to."

Lolly wiped her face. The Geezer Gang would be the death of her.

Cletus pulled the car to the curb while Lance played traffic cop.

"Okay, one at a time. Tell me what happened." A babble of voices greeted her demand.

Lolly gestured at the tourist. "What's your name?"

"Jerry Dennison, and that woman assaulted me." He stabbed a finger at Mee Maw. "I want to press charges."

Oh, no! Mee Maw was about to whack him again.

This wasn't going to work. "Okay. We'll go into the diner, have a cup of coffee and discuss this like adults." Lolly whipped her badge out of her pocket. "And in case anyone wants to disagree, I'm the police chief." She made a shoo-shoo motion with her hands.

"Hey, Chief, what can I get for you folks?" Belle, the owner of the café, rushed to wait on the straggling group.

"Coffee and apple pie all around." Lolly wouldn't even contemplate a food fight.

"Mr. Dennison. I want to hear your version."

Mee Maw almost protested, but Lolly shushed her.

The man was more than happy to give his account. "That…that…that witch hit me with her purse."

Lolly sighed. "Before you go any further, I'd better tell you she's my mother."

He snapped his mouth shut.

Lolly patted Mrs. Pomerantz's hand. "Why don't *you* tell me what happened?"

The white-haired lady smiled. "I was on my way to the Piggly Wiggly. I do that every morning, you know. I like to get the Krispy Kremes while they're fresh." The other seniors nodded in agreement. "They're having a special on rump roast, too."

Her mother began to say something, but Lolly interrupted. "Go ahead with your story, Mrs. Pomerantz."

"Anyway, like I said, I was minding my own business, driving down the street, when all of a sudden that young man ran out in front of my car." She indicated the tourist. "Heavens above. I thought for sure I'd hit him."

Lolly waited for her to continue. "And?"

Mrs. Pomerantz shrugged. "Then he was yanking on my car door and everyone was yelling."

"Let me try this from a different angle. Bill. What did you see?" Lolly asked.

Bill, Mee Maw's strip-poker-playing buddy, pulled off his orange safety vest and put it on the table. "Blinky and I were running the radar gun to catch speeders. We saw Mrs. Pomerantz and decided to shoot her for fun, to see exactly how slow she was driving." He smiled at the woman in question. "It didn't even record on the gun. Anyway, she ran up on the curb and almost clipped that guy." He turned to point at Jerry Dennison. "And the next thing I knew, *he* was out in the street yelling and trying to get her door open."

The man was about to have apoplexy.

"Blinky and I were going to help, but Marcela came out of the diner and took care of things." He shot Mee Maw a goofy grin.

Lolly massaged her temples. "And you must be Blinky." She addressed an elderly Asian man who was also wearing an orange safety vest.

"Colonel Minh Pham, Republic of Vietnam, at your service, madam. But my buddies at Twisted Oaks call me Blinky." The nervous tic was a dead giveaway as to the origin of his nickname. "I can't add much to what Bill told you." He nodded at Mrs. Pomerantz. "She ran up on the sidewalk and then he—" Blinky, too, pointed at the tourist "—tried to jerk her out of the car."

Lolly finally got the picture. She turned to Dennison. "May I see some identification?"

"Why aren't you asking *them* for ID?" Spittle flew from the man's mouth.

"Because I know them." Actually that wasn't quite true. Technically speaking, she'd never been introduced to Blinky, but she'd seen him at Rotary luncheons.

He dug out his wallet and almost threw the license at her.

Lolly examined the photo. "Jerry Dennison. Houston. Hmm." Hopefully Mr. Dennison from the big city wouldn't give her a hard time about the good old-fashioned, small-town justice she was about to administer.

"Mr. Dennison. Tell me your side of the story, why don't you?"

Dennison puffed out his chest. "I was walking down the sidewalk, minding my own business, when that old bat drove up on the curb and tried to kill me." By that time the tourist could barely utter a coherent sentence.

Out of the corner of her eye Lolly saw her mother rise. She was probably getting ready to beat the man senseless. Lolly glared. "Mother!"

She turned back to Dennison. "Were you hit? Are you hurt?"

He frowned. "No, I jumped out of the way."

Lolly suppressed a smile. He was playing right into her hands. "Okay, let me get this straight. You weren't hit, you aren't hurt, but you did attempt to assault one of our senior citizens. Is that correct?"

"Assault. No way! I was trying to talk to the crazy old biddy."

Lolly appeared to be considering his statement. "According to several witnesses, you tried to pull her out of her car. In this town, we view that as assault. I would *strongly* suggest you apologize to these ladies."

His eyes bugged out. "Apologize!"

"Yes. Apologize."

At first she was afraid he'd object, but with a bit of muttering Dennison finally acquiesced. "Sorry."

"If my kids came up with that kind of apology, they'd have to try again. But I guess we'll call it good. Now…" Lolly nodded at the others. "Ladies. It's your turn." Mee Maw had on her stubborn face. "Mother!"

"Oh, all right. Apology accepted." Mee Maw stabbed

a finger at the man and yelled in Mrs. Pomerantz's ear, "He apologized."

Mayberry was alive and well for another day. "Sir, I think you might enjoy your vacation more if you moved down the beach. Don't you?"

Dennison obviously knew when he was outnumbered. He stalked out the front door of the diner as Mee Maw, Bill and Blinky exchanged high-fives.

"Don't gloat, it's not attractive," Lolly admonished. Funny, no one seemed to hear.

Chapter Eleven

Would her life ever get back to normal? An ordinary day of grocery shopping and running kids to soccer practice was sounding like Nirvana. Then when she decided she'd maxed out the weird quotient, the phone rang and it was Wendell.

Okay, that was more than enough! "What do you want, Wendell?"

"Hey, is that any way to talk to your ex?"

"Uh-huh." The man hadn't contacted her in two years, and he had the temerity to want to chat as if they were best friends.

"My band's doing a gig out on Padre Island and I thought you could come out. I have something I need to discuss with you."

She was *not* going to let him irritate her. "We can talk on the phone."

"I think we should reassess the kids and the terms of our divorce."

"What about the kids? You have had visitation rights and you rarely ever come to see them. I refuse to let you disappoint them again." She took a deep breath to remain calm. "Unless you can prove to me you'll be more responsible, I'll pretend you never called."

"A guy can always call his kid, you know. I'll bet my boy would like to talk to me."

And Lolly was afraid he might be right. These days Bren would love to bad-mouth his mother. And no telling what kind of chaos his father could create.

"Okay…" She paused, refusing to get into a fight with him.

"We'll be in town for two days. Come to the club tonight," he said.

What *was* the man up to? Against her better judgment, she muttered, "Where and when?"

"The show starts at nine. I'll be off at eleven." He covered the receiver and spoke to someone. "We're playing at the Sea Shanty on Padre Island. It's the place with the male dancers."

Wasn't that fantastic! "Okay." Lolly hung up and fell into the chair.

"You're not really going to go see that man, are you?" Mee Maw had heard most of the conversation.

"I have to. He's threatening to talk to Bren."

Her mother nodded sagely. "Okay, then call Olivia and get her to go with you. Aunt Sissy and I'll accompany you."

"No!"

"Yes!"

Jeez, would she *ever* win an argument with that woman? Even though Lolly had an amazing arsenal at her disposal—Taser, gun, handcuffs—and the thought of using them on the man was enormously appealing, her mother was her best weapon. Mee Maw terrified Wendell. Always had, always would.

"Okay. Would you call Mrs. Benton and ask her to stay with the kids?" she asked her mother.

When Lolly dialed Olivia to explain the situation, her friend's laughter could've been heard all the way to Corpus.

"THIS IS SOOO exciting." Aunt Sissy adjusted her silver spandex capris. "I've never been to a place where the guys get naked. Except maybe the bathhouse we went to when we were in Paris. Remember that, Marcela?" Mee Maw nodded and grinned.

Lolly's mom resembled a Grape Nehi, decked out from head to toe in purple spandex.

Bathhouses, Paris—those two were certifiably crazy.

Aunt Sissy dug in her purse and came out with a fistful of dollar bills. "I hope I can get close enough to stuff these in their G-strings, or whatever they call them."

Mee Maw and Aunt Sissy were bad enough, but Lolly knew they were in big trouble when Olivia showed up in platform heels and a micromini. She called it her good-hearted-hooker outfit.

Olivia fingered Lolly's shapeless linen blazer. "Not that I'm with the fashion police or anything. But don't you think this is a bit dowdy for a soiree at a strip joint?"

Lolly swatted her hand. "It covers up my holster. And besides that, I'm only going there to talk business." She shooed the women out the door to the Suburban Olivia had borrowed for the trip. "Let's get this over with."

They managed to make it just about a mile before Aunt Sissy insisted on a stop at the Shop and Save. Mee Maw and Aunt Sissy hopped out before Olivia turned off the engine.

The sisters could have been mistaken for twins, and

eccentric didn't even begin to describe them, but Lolly loved them like crazy. With hair that had turned from platinum to silver and the family cornflower-blue eyes, they were darn good-looking, especially for a couple of chicks flirting with seventy.

"Hurry, ladies. We've got to get rolling," Lolly yelled at their retreating backs, even though *hurry* wasn't a word in her mother's vocabulary.

Aunt Sissy returned and stuck her head in the window. "Want anything?"

"Chocolate," Lolly replied.

"Candy or ice cream?"

"Candy."

Olivia jumped out, too. "I've got to hit the little girls' room. Too much coffee."

Lolly wanted to beat her head on the dashboard. Rounding up those three would be like herding cats. Patience, she had to practice patience. Then she heard a familiar roar.

No! No! No! Out of the corner of her eye, she glimpsed a familiar Harley and an even more familiar set of tight male buns. Well, if that didn't beat all—Olivia, Christian and the senior sisters, all in the same convenience store.

Five minutes. Ten minutes. Fifteen minutes. Lolly looked at her watch again. What were they *doing?* Her question was answered when Christian opened the door and escorted the ladies out. And worst of all, they were laughing and chatting like they were the best of friends.

Olivia climbed inside the Suburban and tossed a bag into Lolly's lap. "I have goodies. You, my friend, need some sugar."

Mee Maw and Aunt Sissy opened the back door and giggled. "We invited him."

What! "O-liv-ia!" Each syllable was pronounced separately. "To the bathroom. Now!" They had started the tradition of bathroom summit meetings in junior high school, and most of the major decisions of their young lives had been made in close proximity to the porcelain facilities.

Olivia turned to her coconspirators. "We'll be back."

Lolly started ranting before the door had even closed. "What in heaven's name do you think you're doing inviting that *man* to go with us?"

Olivia put on her obstinate face and Lolly's heart sank. When Livy got that way, she was immovable.

"I asked him because I'd feel safer with a guy along." She put her arm around Lolly's shoulder. "Think about it. We have two adorable, but—" she waved her hands "—iffy senior citizens who want to stuff money in some guy's G-string, and this Sea Shanty place is pretty skuzzy. And there's the fact that we have to contend with Wendell."

Lolly admitted she had a point. "Okay." The evening couldn't get much worse, could it?

Oh, yeah, it could. When they returned to the car, Mee Maw was in the front seat, forcing Lolly into the back with Christian and Aunt Sissy. Not only was she in the backseat, she was in the *middle* of the backseat. Aunt Sissy said she had to have the window because she got carsick. And pigs fly! Lolly knew matchmaking when she saw it.

The way his leg was plastered up against hers, they could have been joined at the hip. That was bad enough, but his arm was also resting on the seat behind her head.

"Scoot over," she hissed.

"Can't." The man had the temerity to grin.

"Lighten up, Lolly." Olivia threw a Snickers bar over the seat.

Lately, it seemed that every time she sat down, he was right there. He was such an irritating man, always touching her—a hand on the elbow, a caress of the cheek. And then there was the kiss. It was *so* annoying.

The Sea Shanty was more than an hour's drive away, and with Christian playing with her ponytail and her relatives acting like love-struck schoolgirls, Lolly was developing a mammoth case of heartburn.

"How long till we get there?" She realized she'd made a major mistake when she heard him chuckle.

"She always did that when she was a kid," Mee Maw piped up. "It about drove her daddy nuts. We'd get in the car to go to San Antonio, and by the time we got to Three Rivers, she'd be hanging out the window claiming she had to upchuck. Just so happened there was a Dairy Queen in Three Rivers, and she'd swear a chocolate shake would settle her tummy."

Olivia apparently had to throw in her two cents' worth. "She did that in high school, too. We couldn't pass a Dairy Queen without stopping. Swear to God, I thought I'd weigh three hundred pounds."

That did it! Lolly turned to her aunt. "Do *you* have anything to add to this discourse?"

"No, dear." She patted Lolly's hand. "I think they can handle it."

"DON'T YOU JUST love Padre?" That comment came from Mee Maw as they passed over the causeway bridge.

In fact, this primitive part of the landscape was one of Lolly's favorite places. The barrier islands running

almost the entire length of the Texas Gulf Coast epito-
mized Mother Nature at her finest. Birds of every hue
and persuasion migrated to the miles of sand dunes to
spend long warm winters basking in the sun.

For years, the only way to drive down Padre Island
was on the packed sands of the beach. It wasn't until the
Padre Island National Seashore was created that roads
were built. A seasonal home to a variety of migratory
birds, sunbaked tourists and spring break revelers, Padre
had somehow managed to maintain its wildness.

On the northern section of the island, development
was limited to several thousand acres near the causeway
bridge at Corpus Christi. It was there that the Sea Shanty
was nestled among the T-shirt shops and motels.

"What self-respecting band would play in a place like
this?" Olivia sounded a bit worried, and no wonder. The
Sea Shanty definitely lived up, or down, to its name. It
was surprising the fire marshal hadn't closed the dump.

"I don't know," Lolly admitted.

At least she didn't have to worry about a bunch of
Bubbas. Quite the opposite—they were more likely to
find giggling, empty-headed females waving money.

And speaking of tittering women, Mee Maw and
Aunt Sissy had already begun the giggle routine.

They paid an outrageous cover charge but were still
escorted to a booth a hundred miles from the stage.

"Should've tipped the host," Christian said, grinning.

Yeah, yeah, yeah. Mee Maw and Aunt Sissy looked
distressed, and Olivia could barely keep a straight face.

"All right, all right!" Lolly marched back to the front
and waved a twenty. Voilà, they had a table near the
stage. Christian scooted his seat up so close to hers she
could practically hear his heartbeat.

"This is so exciting." Aunt Sissy laid her wad of dollar bills on the table.

Exciting wasn't exactly how Lolly would've described it. Interesting, educational or—if she stretched it—maybe even entertaining. She'd never seen so many half-naked, oiled-up, buff-looking guys in her life. They ran the gamut from firemen and cops to cowboys, construction workers and motorcycle jocks. Or at least their costumes did—what there was of them. And bless their little pea-pickin' hearts, Mama and Aunt Sissy were right up front waving their money.

When it was time for the band to fire up, Lolly remembered why Wendell hadn't made the varsity marching band. He should've stuck with his day job. After they finished playing, Wendell strolled over. Jeez—the guy acted like the king of the world.

"You guys keep your mouths zipped, you hear me?" Lolly insisted. "Particularly you." She poked a finger at Christian.

He smiled, but held up his hands in a sign of surrender.

"Gag me with a fork," Olivia commented as Wendell paused to schmooze some band groupies.

Wendell nodded at the ladies and pulled up a chair from an adjoining table. "Miz Hamilton, Miz Phillips. Did you enjoy the show?" He tried to kiss Lolly's cheek, but missed when she moved back. "Olivia. Long time, no see."

"Not long enough," Olivia muttered under her breath and was rewarded by her friend with a kick to the shin.

Lolly put her elbows on the table and leaned forward. "Let's get down to business. Exactly what is your agenda?"

He tilted his chair back on two legs. "I want to have a private conversation with you."

Oh, what she wouldn't give to shove that chair the tiniest bit. God, when *had* she acquired those violent tendencies?

"Won't happen," she said blandly. "Anything you want to say, you can say in front of these folks. I want witnesses."

He screwed his face into the pout Lolly remembered well. "I'm quitting this gig and coming back to Port Serenity."

That was not something she wanted to hear.

"So when I'm in town, I figure I'll run into my kids every once in a while."

Lolly lifted an eyebrow. "You have a legal right to some specific visitation opportunities. Do you plan to keep them?"

He plopped the chair down on the floor. "Sure, regular as clockwork. My old buddy Jamison says Bren needs a guy in his life. Rumor has it he's running wild."

When she saw Jamison she was going to perform a lobotomy on him with a dull steak knife! "If I let you see them, can you promise you won't do anything to get them in trouble, especially Bren? He's at an impressionable age."

Wendell displayed an oily smile. "I'm an expert on teenagers, ya know."

Yeah, she knew. Olivia was tapping her fingernails, her mother looked like she was about to use her purse as an assault weapon and Christian was ominously quiet.

It took a superhuman effort, but Lolly managed to smile. "Assuming you actually show up, we're setting some ground rules. If you get Bren in even the slightest bit of trouble, I'll go back to court and make sure you never see them again. Do you get my drift?"

He gave her a sickly grin. "Yep, I get it." He tipped an imaginary hat and sauntered off.

Lolly took a deep breath. "That went well for a first skirmish, don't you think?"

Christian's guffaw broke the silence.

"Did you see the look on his face?" Olivia asked. "Guess you never threatened him before."

"Me? Threaten him? I'm an officer of the court. I wouldn't threaten anyone."

"Hey, I'm your best friend and I wouldn't tangle with you when it comes to your kids. But Wendell's not a brain trust."

Christian took her hand and was encouraged when Lolly didn't pull away. A range of emotions played across her face as she studied their entwined fingers.

No wonder—she was probably as confused as he was. For him, it was an unfamiliar minefield of protective feelings. Lust he'd felt before—maybe not quite this strong—but the protective thing was new. Mr. Wendell LaTullipe required a little background check. No telling what that would turn up.

OLIVIA WATCHED the sparks between Lolly and Christian with interest. Those two could light up the Gulf Coast. And if she didn't miss her guess, Miss Stubborn would deny the attraction with her last breath. Silly woman!

Their sisterhood had been forged in the fires of a hard-fought spelling bee in the seventh grade, and had endured for almost twenty years. No doubt about it, their friendship was rock-solid. So why wasn't Lolly confiding in her? And why wasn't she admitting, even to herself, that she was smitten?

Chapter Twelve

Olivia's birthday was on Saturday, and because the birth-day girl got to choose the party, Lolly was stuck with a trip to Cotton-Eyed Joe's country-and-western dance hall. Frankly, she'd rather have a Brazilian bikini wax.

"Why aren't you ready?" Olivia sashayed into the kitchen. "Bustle it up. Get out of those public service duds and pour on some party clothes." She indicated the hall to the bedrooms.

"Livy's right." Speaking to Lolly, Mee Maw winked at Olivia. "See how pretty she is."

Olivia did look like a million bucks in her tight white jeans, silk Western shirt, boots and Stetson. But that was Olivia's style; Lolly would look like a dork in that getup.

"Every man in the place is going to want to dance with her," Mee Maw commented. And that wasn't all they'd want to do with her.

Lolly sighed, but she knew when she was out-gunned and outnumbered, so she might as well go down gracefully.

Olivia got right in her face. "Make it short, tight and sexy. I don't want to be seen with a frump. Don't even consider coming out here in baggy pants and a blazer."

Lolly blew her friend a raspberry. If her mother hadn't been sitting there, she would've been more explicit.

She was a mother, a cop, a member of the Chamber of Commerce. What did she know about short, tight and sexy?

Lolly dug through her closet until she found a denim skirt and a red T-shirt. They weren't exactly short or tight but they'd have to do.

"Get your butt out here," Olivia yelled down the hall. "We have some dancin' to do. If you're not here in three seconds, I'm going to come back there and get you."

"I'm coming, I'm coming. Get a grip." Lolly grabbed a pair of red stiletto heels and her red hand-tooled cowboy boots. Time for advice from the fashion mavens.

"Okay, what do you think?" She put on one of each.

"Boots. You won't even be able to walk in those things," Olivia said, pointing at the shoes, "much less dance."

"Definitely the boots," her mother concurred. "Have fun, girls, and don't worry about a thing."

Olivia swatted Lolly's butt and broke into peals of giggles. "Don't get in a worried snit. Robstown is far enough away that we're not going to see anyone we know. And you're gorgeous. We're both gorgeous."

COTTON-EYED JOE's dance hall was a local landmark on the edge of town, next to the cotton gin. Cotton's, as it was known by the locals, didn't set a whole lot of store on ambiance or amenities. A corrugated roof kept the rain out. The wooden sides could be raised to let in the breeze. And the dance floor was swept once a week, whether it was needed or not. Yikes!

Cotton's only concession to the modern world was its sound system. And when the speakers were cranked up, it could out-decibel the space launch. Lolly's ears already hurt—and she was out in the parking lot. She'd give fifty bucks for a pair of earplugs.

"There's a bunch of cowboys here tonight." Olivia trolled the parking area for almost twenty minutes before she found an empty space.

"Tell me something, Livy. How often do you come here?"

Olivia stopped the four-by-four and frowned at Lolly. "I've never been here before. Why do you ask?"

"Because I'm not sure it's safe. Check it out." Lolly waved her hand at the parking lot. "Pickups with rifle racks, Harleys, eighteen-wheelers and a couple of battered SUVs. Do you see a nice safe Buick sedan anywhere?"

"Lighten up, Lolly." Funny, this wasn't the first time she'd heard that.

Lolly ignored both her comment and the catcalls they were getting from a group of young men. "And do you see any, and I mean any, unaccompanied women going in that door?" The door in question was open and an old George Strait tune was blasting across the asphalt. Lolly was afraid of hearing damage, and she wasn't within a hundred yards of the joint.

"Stop being such a spoilsport. Come on." Olivia pulled her toward the den of iniquity.

"Are you sangle?" The ticket-taker was sporting a cowboy hat the size of Dallas.

"What did you say?" Lolly shouted.

"Are you sangle?" he shouted back.

Olivia grabbed Lolly's money and shoved it at the guy. "Yes. We're both single."

He smiled as he ogled them. "Yes, ma'am. Y'all have a good time, now, ya hear. Lemme stamp your hand."

Lolly really didn't want a big red stamp on the top of her hand, but she held it out for him to make his imprint.

"I'm only doing this because I love you. You know that, don't you," she screamed at Olivia. Screaming was the only way she could be heard over the music.

"Gotcha. Let's go find a table. Away from the speakers." Olivia strolled toward the rear of the dance hall. "Looks like there are some over there."

There were also some skanky people back there, and Lolly wished she'd picked up her stun gun. Half the population of Aransas County was out on the minuscule dance floor, stomping and swaying in a seemingly choreographed circle.

"Do you know how to do that?" Lolly indicated the guys and gals pivoting, rocking and kicking in unison.

"No, but I'm sure we can find some good-looking dude who'd be willing to teach us."

And that was exactly what Lolly was afraid of. She hadn't missed all the looks they were getting from the "sangle" guys. Lord help her!

Olivia punched her arm and pulled her toward a table.

"We'll have two draft Lone Stars," Olivia yelled to a waitress who appeared almost as soon as they sat down. "Now we just wait to see which of these guys hits on us first," she mouthed as she turned to grace the aforementioned males with one of her killer smiles. Six of them almost expired on the spot.

Before Lolly could blink, four men crowded around the small table.

While Olivia made eyes at a tall, dark cowboy in a large Stetson, Lolly chose the one with red hair and freckles who looked like Howdy Doody.

"I don't know how to do that." She pointed at the dancers.

"Don't worry about it. I'll teach you." And he did. Before she knew it, she was doing a reasonable semblance of the Texas Schottische, the El Paso and the Cotton-Eyed Joe. So far she hadn't maimed anyone, and that was saying a lot.

Lolly was having a ball and the number of cowboys lining up to dance with her spanned the range of body types and ages: tall, short, skinny, beer guts, old, young and in-between. What they all had in common was boots, a shiny rodeo belt buckle and a big Stetson.

"Oh, my gosh, I'm having a great time." Olivia had ditched her latest suitor.

Lolly shooed off another potential dance partner.

"Are you having a good time?" Olivia asked.

Lolly tugged the damp T-shirt and fanned. She was dying of heat and took a gulp of beer. "How long has this swill been sitting here?" Lolly seriously considered spitting out the lukewarm brew. "And yes, I'm having a great time. Much as I hate to admit it, I'm glad you dragged me along."

Since the band was taking a break, the noise level had diminished. When Olivia ordered another round, Lolly checked out her surroundings. This was the south Texas version of an L.A. meat market. She was a mother, for goodness sake—moms didn't do bar scenes. So why *was* she here?

IT WAS C.J.'S FAULT they were at Cotton's—he claimed Christian needed to get out more. But what was *her* excuse?

"If that twit doesn't get his tongue back in his mouth,

I'm going to rip it out for him. It'll be mighty hard to swallow if he doesn't have a tongue."

C.J. took a draw on his longneck. "Yeah, boss, mighty hard."

"What's so funny?" Christian snapped. "That cowboy's eyes about popped out of his head when she did that fanning thing with her T-shirt. Probably thought he'd died and gone to heaven." And Christian knew just how he felt. Before his brain engaged long enough to stop him, he found himself stomping over to their table.

"Wait up. I'm right behind you," C.J. called as he followed Christian. People parted like the Red Sea.

"Hold up, just a minute." C.J. grabbed his arm. "What *exactly* have you got in mind?"

Now that was a good question. What *was* he going to do? Coldcock a cowboy? Hammer a hormone-driven post-adolescent college kid? No—definitely not. He was a professional. He worked with logic and reason. Ha! Not when it came to that blond-haired beauty. Something about her brought out the caveman in him. Christian closed in on his target.

He leaned over until he was almost nose-to-nose with Lolly. "Are you trying to start a riot?"

Lolly's heart beat rapidly when she realized who it was. Then she was irked by his comment. "Not that it's any of your business, but I'm out dancing. What are you doing here?"

He could see the sparks in her blue eyes. On a conscious level, Christian knew he didn't want to make her mad, but he couldn't seem to control his mouth.

"C.J. dragged me here, but that's not the point." He waved a hand at her T-shirt. "Every guy in the place was ogling…that."

If the fiery daggers she was shooting him were any indication, he had about thirty-three seconds to live.

C.J. sidled up to Olivia as Christian continued to make a fool of himself. The band had returned and launched the new set with a slow number. "Let's dance." Christian stood and pulled Lolly up with him. Despite the heat and exercise, she had her own unique smell—a blend of sunshine and ripe peaches. He couldn't tell whether it was her perfume, her soap or her shampoo. It was all he could do not to nuzzle her neck and take a deep breath.

He urged her toward the dance floor, where several couples swayed to the music. The girls had their thumbs hooked in the guys' belt loops, and most of the guys had at least one hand firmly attached to a feminine bottom.

When he put his arms around her waist, Lolly twined hers around his neck and laid her head on his chest. She was lush and ripe; her curves and soft skin were all woman. Waves of heat radiated from her body, and when she gave a soft little sigh he just about lost it. They were melded together from chest to thigh, so she had to notice his obvious arousal.

Christian rubbed his hands up and down her arms and fantasized about dipping his fingers into the lacy cups of her bra that peeked over the low V of her T-shirt. He closed his eyes and let his hands slide past her rib cage to the dip of her waist and then they meandered down to rest on her round and very firm derriere. The cowboys had this one right.

Drops of sweat formed on his upper lip as Christian tried to tame his Mr. Happy. Every brain cell was fried. This woman was trouble with a capital *T*—she was commitment, kids and fluffy cats. But was that such a bad idea? She was also an aphrodisiac he couldn't resist.

Christian ached to tangle his fingers in her hair and kiss her senseless. He started at the hollow of her neck, then worked his way up her neck with a string of hot kisses. He didn't care if this was a public place. His sensory system was on overload. One more taste of her sweet mouth—that was all he wanted. He was about to reach the ultimate goal when his cell phone vibrated.

"Not now!" he muttered but checked the text message. He and C.J. were supposed to report to the captain's office in Houston. ASAP! That could only mean big trouble. "We have to go. I'll call you and let you know when I'll be back." Christian kissed the end of her nose. The next time he kissed her mouth, he intended to have her full attention and a nice soft bed.

"Let's get it rolling," Christian barked at his partner.

C.J. reluctantly followed even though his attention was on another beautiful woman. He gave Olivia a dimpled grin.

C.J. STUDIED Christian as he stomped off. The guy was one of the toughest street-smart guys around, but this time he'd met his match—blond, blue-eyed and curvaceous. Who would ever have guessed it?

LOLLY STOOD motionless on the dance floor as the men left. What in the world had happened?

Olivia joined her. "You two looked like you were about to go up in flames."

Lolly shook her head. "Oh, boy, you don't know the half of it."

Chapter Thirteen

Sand and sagebrush stretched as far as the eye could see. The only sign of human habitation was a cluster of rusted single-wide trailers.

"I'm sick to death of this." Christian adjusted the night-vision goggles as he crawled on his belly to the next cactus.

"Yeah," C.J. whispered over the radio. "And if that rattler doesn't stop trying to cozy up to me, I'm going to blow his stinkin' head off."

Christian shifted to a larger clump of prickly pear and focused on the perimeter chain-link fence topped with razor wire. "All I see from here is a javelina hog. If we're lucky, he'll play havoc with their motion detector."

"I'd hate to be an illegal and run across these dudes," C.J. commented.

"Isn't that the truth?" Christian wondered how many illegals had wandered too close to the camp. More than likely, they hadn't lived to tell the tale.

For the past three nights, Christian and his team of narcs had parked four miles away and trudged in to stake out a compound they were certain was a major methamphetamine lab. But before they went in, they had to assess what they were up against.

In a part of the world where ranches went on for thousands of acres, isolation could be used as a first line of defense for drug dealers. Approaching vehicles could be spotted miles away by their rooster tail of dirt. Reconnaissance during the daylight hours was a virtual impossibility. So the good guys were forced to provide nocturnal company for the snakes and scorpions that called this moonscape home.

A man on the other side of the compound keyed his radio. "Guys, there's a truck coming from the west."

This was the first activity the team had seen since they'd started the surveillance.

"How many people?" Christian asked.

"Two. Think this is the connection we've been waiting for?"

Christian hoped so. It was half past midnight, and all the trailers, with the exception of one, were dark. Someone in the mobile home was undoubtedly brewing up meth. The hum of a generator and the engine of the approaching truck broke the stillness of the desert night.

Christian was watching the gate when the trailer with the light on went up in a ball of flames.

He could hear expletives from all his men, who were wearing night-vision goggles. The flash of light had temporarily blinded them.

Christian jumped to his feet and raced toward the perimeter. In order to salvage the mission, they had to use the blast as a diversion. "Showtime," Christian yelled. "We're going in!" If only he knew what kind of firepower they were facing. Without a doubt, the bad guys were armed to the teeth. He adjusted his night-vision goggles and ran into the fray.

A barechested man in a pair of unbuttoned jeans ran out of the trailer and was tackled by one of Christian's men. The armed lawmen stopped the pickup as it tried to speed off into the sagebrush.

Another thunderous explosion and an accompanying blast of searing wind almost knocked Christian off his feet. A propane tank blew and the fire spread to the next building.

The second detonation created an exodus of people from the compound. "Police! On the ground! Get on the ground! Now! Get on the ground!" The commands were punctuated by an escalating series of explosions.

A man with a semiautomatic ran toward the razor wire and freedom.

"Don't try it." C.J. aimed his assault rifle and yelled, "Drop it and get on your knees."

The man threw down his gun and as he fell to the ground a truck gas tank blew with a deafening roar.

When the furor died down, C.J. jerked off his Kevlar vest and tossed it on the hard, dry earth.

"Do you think we're even going to make a dent?"

C.J's question went straight to the heart of Christian's discontent. It felt euphoric to bust a lab. And getting the scumbags off the street made his day. But he was beginning to think he was too old and jaded to continue the fieldwork. He surveyed the compound where the dregs of society produced a drug guaranteed to ruin lives.

"I don't know, I just don't know."

Chapter Fourteen

Christian watched her through the screen. Harvey thumped his tail and displayed a doggy grin when he bothered to raise his head at all. Dribbles of slobber rested in the corners of his mouth as his furry tail beat a tattoo in welcome. And he was supposed to be a watchdog?

Lolly was up to her elbows in suds washing dishes, singing and swaying to a Faith Hill tune. She was adorable in her white shorts, halter top and ponytail all askew. How long would it take her to realize she wasn't alone? As a cop, her vulnerability disturbed him, but as a male he reveled in the time it gave him to feast on the sight.... What he was about to do was a huge mistake, but he was going to do it anyway. His soul desperately needed it. He opened the screen door. Harvey butted his hand in welcome, then plopped down again.

Some small noise alerted her that she had company. The hair stood up on the back of her neck as she carefully gripped the butcher knife she'd been washing. Her holster was locked in the desk. The knife was the best she could do on a moment's notice. Lolly slowly turned around. On one level she was relieved when she saw her visitor in his black T-shirt and tight jeans. There was no physical danger from this man, but she was afraid he presented an even greater threat.

"Are the kids here?" he asked. She managed to shake her head.

"Are they coming back anytime soon?" Another shake.

"They're both at sleepovers." That admission came as she realized she was still holding the knife. It dripped suds all over her bare feet, but she didn't notice the pool of water. Incapable of coherent speech, she watched him close the wooden door and lock it with a deafening click. If she didn't say something soon, she wouldn't be able to back out.

He walked toward her. She'd wondered how a man that big could move that quietly. Before he reached the sink, he unhooked the Velcro holster strapped to his leg and set the gun on the kitchen table. It seemed out of place next to the vase of daisies.

"I need you." That was all he said before he took the knife. He splayed his hands across her back and waited for her reaction. Did he expect consent or merely acquiescence? Ah, there was a God. Her eyes shimmered with unshed tears. She wanted this as much as he did. He unfastened her ponytail and ran his fingers through her hair as he feasted on her mouth. Little nibbles. Deep, wet kisses.

He seemed ravenous and Lolly simply wanted to get into his skin with him. She wasn't nearly close enough as he delved into her soul. A troop of Girl Scouts could've been having a campout in the kitchen and she wouldn't have cared. Cogent moments were few.

Somewhere far, far away she could hear Faith singing about a kiss. That girl didn't know nothin'. Now *this* was a kiss.

He maneuvered her from the sink to the wall and bracketed her hands above her head while he savored her mouth and her neck. This was well beyond anything Lolly had ever experienced. He put his leg between her thighs and gently rocked back and forth.

He kissed his way down to her cleavage and made the return voyage back to her mouth. Slow, hot kisses that drove her mad. He paid homage to every one of the freckles sprinkled across her chest.

With his free hand he untied the top of the halter, and when the cloth fell forward the back tie met the same fate.

In response she ran her fingers through his silky dark hair as he moved from one breast to the other—molding, licking, kissing, sucking. Lolly could barely draw a breath. If this was foreplay, she wasn't sure she'd survive the main course.

He had to let go of her hands as he nibbled and licked his way to the waistband of her shorts. The zipper slid down silently, and miraculously the shorts and bikinis disappeared just as the halter had. The man knew how to get a woman out of her clothes. But wait a minute, he was fully clothed and she didn't have on a stitch. Not fair—incredibly sensual, but definitely not fair. Before she could rectify the situation, he continued his foray even farther south and every thought other than lust went right out of her head.

She didn't even recognize herself as she clutched his head and made strangled noises. The most intimate of all mating lasted an eternity—or perhaps just a few moments—then he stood and resumed his exploration of her mouth.

"Bed?" It was hoarse but understandable.

Where was the closest bed? She could barely remember her own name. There was a guest room off the kitchen—it had a bed. Whether it was big or small, soft or hard, didn't matter; it was close. Lolly grabbed a fistful of T-shirt and pulled him down the hall. She vaguely noticed that he was shedding his clothes before they made it to the door. When the back of her knees hit the edge of the bed, she'd yanked the remaining piece of clothing over his head. They landed on the mattress in a tangle of arms and legs, and time ceased to exist. Blackout or utter bliss—nothing mattered. Not beepers, kids, corpses, scumbags or ex-husbands. Nothing was important except losing themselves in each other.

Her heart pounded like a marimba band, she was light-headed and it was hard to breathe. Just as she decided she was having a heart attack, Christian nestled between her legs and then she *knew* she was going to self-combust. "Do it! Just *do* it! I'm dying!"

"Yes, ma'am. Happy to oblige." But instead he rolled off her and searched for his jeans, and the tiny packet he had stashed in his wallet.

Lolly wanted to scream in frustration, but she soon found out it was worth the wait.

The way he stroked the tender skin of her inner thighs was so… He was studying her—and the slightest smile lurked at his lips. Suddenly the playfulness stopped.

Their sweat-slicked bodies rubbed against each other as he pressed her into the mattress. His crisp chest hair rubbed against her breasts. And then he pushed slowly into her and she forgot everything else.

THE CLOCK HAD chimed midnight and Lolly was asleep, curled up like a contented kitten, her blond hair spread across the pillow. Christian levered himself up on one elbow and marveled at how much he wanted her. The tan-line accentuated her creamy white breasts as they rose and fell softly.

He reluctantly admitted he was experiencing a fight-or-flight reflex. The woman was addictive. She was the living, breathing epitome of home and hearth—and hot, sweaty sex.

Christian was afraid he'd made a mistake of mammoth proportions. He'd fallen head over heels in love with this woman, and it scared him witless.

He *had* to get out of there and think, but he couldn't resist one last kiss. She didn't even stir as he quietly stole away. She was going to be furious when she woke up and realized he was gone. He took a final look as she rolled over and sighed. Then he crept out of the room and grabbed his holster from the kitchen table. He stopped at the door and as he flipped the lock, he saw Harvey. "Take care of your mom, big boy," he whispered.

"You no-good, sorry, pond-scum jerk!"

Christian cracked open one eye. He remembered leaving Lolly asleep. He remembered trudging back to his bleak apartment and falling into bed. But he didn't remember giving the golden Valkyrie straddling his chest a key to his place.

"And a good morning to you, gorgeous. Are you always so cranky the morning after?" He really had to do something about that death wish. She was a goddess of war with her riotous golden hair and sky-blue eyes shooting sparks.

"How dare you!" Lolly leaned over his chest until their noses almost touched. "How *dare* you come over for an easy lay and then sneak out!" She drew back and struck his chest with her fist.

"Whoa! That hurt." He grabbed her hands and anchored them against him with one hand.

He clamped his other hand on the back of her neck and tugged her down until he could see the tiny flecks of green in her eyes. "Lady, you are anything but easy! I'll admit I had a bit of a flight reflex. Frankly, you scare the crap out of me." Pausing, he whispered, "I'm sorry I left." He threaded his fingers through her hair and pulled her even closer. Her breath was coming in short pants—as if she was having a hard time getting enough oxygen.

So was he.... This was *such* a bad idea, but Christian was going to do it anyway.

He urged her down until she molded to his body. That was exactly where she was supposed to be. Oh, yeah, her smell, her taste, her silkiness, they were meant for him—and him alone.

Christian slid his hands under her T-shirt, up over her rib cage to the full roundness of her breasts. Then he reversed their positions and slid down her running shorts and her panties. "Miss Lolly, you're killing me," he growled and flipped her over onto her stomach. "Now, gorgeous, I think we're ready for something different." He pulled her up on her hands and knees. "This is something I've wanted to do ever since I saw you in that bar."

The wet, hot kisses he trailed down her spine made her legs feel like melted butter. Could they hold her up? Was the man trying to torture her? If pure pleasure was painful, he was a sadist of the highest magnitude. As he moved back up to her neck he entered her and Lolly's world erupted in fireworks worthy of a Fourth of July celebration.

"I DON'T EVEN LIKE YOU." That was one of the biggest lies she'd ever told. Her backside was snuggled up against his groin and the hand he had draped over her waist was entertaining itself by playing with her nipple.

"Well, I like you. A lot."

She could feel him chuckle and then nibble on her neck.

"And how did you get in here, anyway?" he asked.

"I picked the lock."

"The police chief is guilty of breaking and entering." He brought a hand to his chest. "I'm not sure my heart can take this."

"Oh, puleeze!" She wiggled and was rewarded for her efforts. "I only have an hour before Amanda gets home."

"Enough time," he insisted. "Definitely enough time."

Chapter Fifteen

Lolly swatted Christian when he kissed the nape of her neck.

"Don't do that. This is a police station and there are people working here."

Christian leaned closer. "So there are." He whispered, "That big desk of yours is giving me ideas."

It was all too much. She was trying to work while he made erotic and highly tempting suggestions about the things they could do on her desk. She'd never look at that piece of furniture in the same way. Oh, brother!

Then Mayor Lance tapped on the door and stuck his head in. So much for unfulfilled sexual fantasies.

"Lolly, I hate to interrupt, but we need to talk to you." He looked sheepish and she wondered how much of the conversation he'd overheard.

"Come on in. You aren't interrupting anything." Christian took the hint and wandered toward his desk.

Precious followed her dad into the office. "We need to talk to you *privately*." Lance gestured surreptitiously at Christian, who was pecking at the computer as if he had an important document to finish.

"It's okay to talk in front of Lieutenant Delacroix."

"Well." Lance paused. "If you're sure. Precious has something to tell you."

Just what she needed—a teenage confession. "Yes, Precious. What can I do for you?"

Precious, hell-raiser supreme, was uncharacteristically subdued.

"I was at a party out at the quay last night. You know, college kids, stuff like that." She looked at her dad for support. "Anyway, there was some drinking, and you know, like necking and stuff. A couple of guys had some weed."

So far, nothing she said was surprising. Lolly had heard rumors about the beach parties, but they hadn't been able to snag any of the participants yet.

"Well, anyway. Since you got me out of the Peaceful Cove mess that time, I figured I should tell you."

Lolly's patience was being sorely tried, but she kept her voice calm and easy. "What do you want to tell me?"

Precious sighed. "Bren and his buddies were there last night, and they brought most of the beer. He told a couple of kids that his dad bought it for him. Everybody got pretty sloshed."

"What?" *Control!* She had to stay in control, and she really should breathe. "His dad!" Inhale, exhale. "Are you absolutely positive it was Bren?"

"Yes, ma'am. I've known him since he was in diapers. He kinda stands out in a crowd."

Unfortunately, she was right. The kid was too attractive for his own good.

Lolly didn't want to ask, but she had to know. "Was he doing grass?"

"No, ma'am, just beer." Precious giggled. "He's really cute, even if he is, like, *so* young."

Lolly turned to the mayor. "Lance, did you realize Wendell was back in town?"

He shrugged. "Yeah. I think he has an apartment over at the Seven Seas."

Lolly rubbed her temples. "Thanks, Precious. You did the right thing and that takes a lot of guts."

She suspected Lance felt vindicated. For once his kid wasn't on the hot seat. Hers was.

Lance gave Lolly a brotherly hug. "We're going. It'll be okay." He walked out, trailed by Precious who stared at Christian all the way out the door.

Her first inclination was to ground the kid until he was thirty-five, but that wasn't very realistic. What was she going to do?

Lolly resisted the urge to bang her head on the desk.

"So what's your plan?" Christian asked, echoing her own question.

"I'm thinking, I'm thinking."

"You want me to take care of this?"

She reluctantly shook her head. "No. I have to deal with it." She massaged her neck. "I thought he was spending the night with Jason, but I'd bet my pension that Jason was supposed to be spending the night at our house."

Lolly flipped open her Rolodex and found Jason's number. Bingo—the kids had pulled the old spend-the-night-with-a-buddy scam.

With a little luck and a lot of patience, Lolly discovered that five of Bren's buddies were also missing in action. But where were they? Then she hit pay dirt. One of the kids had chickened out and was at home. A couple of well-placed comments, and the kid squealed. The boys had spent the night at Wendell's parents' beach house.

Lolly paced the office until she came up with an idea.

"Joe," she called down the hall. "Would you get Cletus and come in here? I need some help." She turned to Christian. "If you're willing, I want you involved, too."

He smiled. "Yes, ma'am. Always glad to help a beautiful woman."

"Not that. I need you to be scary."

"Oh, I can do that, too."

Which was the understatement of the century.

Joe sat in the only empty chair and Cletus lounged against the doorsill while Lolly outlined her plan. "I'll call all the parents and get their permission. Joe, can you have everything in place in thirty minutes? I want the little twits to be asleep when we arrive." Lolly planned to scare her baby boy out of a couple of months' growth. Then she'd deal with Wendell.

AN IMPRESSIVE CONVOY of police vehicles made its way out to the LaTullipes' secluded beach house. Christian rode with Lolly in her Blazer, while Joe and Cletus each drove a cruiser.

The beach where the LaTullipe family had their summer cottage was a popular hangout for bonfires, wiener roasts and general rowdiness. The narrow spit of land provided the perfect privacy for illicit keggers. Wendell and his buddies had used it all during high school.

It had been a long time since Lolly had visited the beach house, but she found the sandy drive without much trouble. The house was a weather-beaten shingled affair built on stilts to survive hurricane tidal surges.

She turned off the flashing lights before she pulled up to the back of the house. Joe and Cletus joined them at the bottom of the stairs. "Here's the plan," Lolly said.

"We're going in like a SWAT team, lots of noise. No weapons. We're going to scare the hell out of those little idiots."

Joe nodded. He had five kids of his own, so he was game for anything. "We can do that."

The group quietly crept up the wooden stairs, and when Lolly nodded, Christian took over. He crashed through the door and bellowed at the top of his lungs. "Police!" The kids scattered like cockroaches.

"Stay right where you are. Every one of you." Lolly used her best "don't give me any nonsense" voice.

Bren peeked over the back of the couch. "Mommmmmm?"

Lolly ignored her son. "Every one of you, line up over here." She counted five kids cowering in the living room and another four who scurried in from the bedroom. Thank goodness all the hooligans were boys. Girls would have complicated her plan. Not to mention the fact that her mom radar would've gone into overdrive.

"If any of you can prove you're twenty-one, step forward. We have a special prize for you." No one moved. She gave them the evil eye. "Get your shorts on." Kids scrambled for their clothes. "I want to see ID from everyone. Now!" Wallets magically appeared.

"Mom!" Since Bren and his buddies were too young to drive, they only had school ID cards. The evil eye was all it took to forestall anything else he had to say.

Two of the boys were seventeen and two were eighteen. "You guys." She spoke to the eighteen-year-olds. "Call your parents. Tell them you're going to be occupied, along with your friends—" she made a waving motion around the room "—digging ditches for the new park irrigation system. You two, give me your phone numbers. I'm calling your parents. And the rest of you, I've already talked to your folks."

One of the older boys piped up. "You can't make us do that."

Lolly smiled. "Planning to be a lawyer, huh? You're an underage drinker and you're guilty of trespass. The people who own this house didn't give any of you permission to spend the night. I talked to them. So, you have two choices. Dig ditches or spend some quality time in my jail, or juvie hall for the minors." She put on one of her nastiest smirks. "Just consider this a teenage chain gang." That effectively put an end to any objections.

"Mom, I'm sick." Bren seemed a bit green, but Lolly hardened her heart.

"Do I look like I care?" This was going to be harder on her than on Bren, but he wouldn't appreciate it until he had his own kids.

She shooed the boys out the door. "Half of you go with Sergeant Joe, and the rest of you get in Officer Taylor's car."

Lolly heard Sergeant Joe ask his captives if they'd ever seen the old movie *Cool Hand Luke.* They'd be working their butts off for the next couple of days, and if that didn't make an impression, she didn't know what would.

Joe leaned on the top of his cruiser and winked at her. "I'll watch them like a hawk and make sure they do a good job."

"Have lots of ice water and feed them, too. You can take it out of my budget."

Joe nodded. "Don't worry about a thing, boss. They'll be fine. I'll have someone drive 'em home when we're finished for the day."

Christian walked around to the driver's side after.

"I'm your chauffeur, and I'm taking you out for coffee. You seem a little frazzled."

Lolly felt horrible and probably looked worse. She tossed him the keys thinking he'd drive to Daisy's Diner; instead, he headed out toward the highway.

"Where are we going?"

"Nueces Pass. I've heard of this great place for a chocolate milkshake," he answered. "I think that's just what you need."

She couldn't help wincing. He remembered the embarrassing stories about the Dairy Queen and the chocolate milkshakes. But he was right. She needed a thick chocolate shake and a good cry, and not necessarily in that order. Kids had a way of standing your world on its ear without even realizing it.

Christian whipped into the parking lot of the Tastee Freeze. They had the best shakes in the county, even better than the Dairy Queen.

He led her to a small lawn dotted with picnic tables. "Find us a place to sit and I'll order. You want a large?"

She nodded and wandered off across the grass. The sounds of summer in south Texas enveloped her—cicadas chirping, kids squealing in play and wind sighing through the trees. These were the lazy, hazy, crazy days of summer, but she was just plain miserable.

Christian sat down next to her on the bench. "Here you go, gorgeous." He took a slurp. "You know he's just being a kid, don't you?"

That was all it took. Big tears spilled down her cheeks. No matter how many times she told herself to stop the waterworks, the tears kept flowing.

"Oh, sweetheart, come here." He removed the cup from Lolly's hand and plunked her onto his lap.

She'd never been one of those lucky girls who cried dainty little tears without so much as smudging her mascara. No, siree, she went for the gusto—raccoon eyes, clown nose, red face—and it was a scary, scary sight! She didn't cry very often, and she never cried in public. So why was she sitting in this guy's lap bawling like a baby?

And speaking of mascara, she'd managed to get makeup all over his T-shirt. "Um, your shirt is wet and it has gook on it."

He ran the pad of his thumb under her eye. "No problem, it's black. Just don't blow your nose on it."

That elicited a watery laugh.

He continued to rub her back. "I'm not very good when women cry."

She hiccupped and burrowed her face in his chest. "You could've fooled me. Is anyone watching us?" She didn't want an audience for her momentary lapse of sanity.

"The varsity cheerleading squad was here, but they beat feet when you started bawling."

She bit him on the neck.

"Ow! What did you do that for?" He rubbed his neck. "There was an old lady with a schnauzer but she left when there wasn't any action," he said, amending his statement.

Since she didn't have a paper bag handy, she'd have to look him in the eye sooner or later. No time like the present. She lifted her head and dared him to laugh. Smart man, he obviously had a will of iron.

"Scary," he said as he gave in to a tilt of the lip.

Maybe he wasn't as smart as he appeared. She wiped at the mascara.

Christian produced a clean handkerchief. "Let me. You're smearing it." He wiped under her eyes. "Now blow."

She felt about three years old, but it was wonderfully comforting.

She put her head back on his chest, not ready to face the world yet.

"Better?"

"A little."

"Want to talk about it?"

Come to think of it, she did. "Sometimes I feel like the lousiest mother in south Texas. Then other times, I *know* I'm the lousiest mother."

Christian kissed the top of her head. "Oh, darlin'. You're a great mother. The kid's a teenager. It's his job to get in trouble now and then. I'd be more worried if he was a nerdy loner. They either become billionaires or torture cats. Kids like Bren become cops and doctors."

"Not a cop."

"Okay, no cops or lawyers." He adjusted her position on his lap. "Seriously, you did a great job this morning. If that didn't scare those kids they're not scare-able. Most of 'em were about ready to mess their drawers."

"I hope I did the right thing. The parents I talked to were all for it. It terrifies me to think about the trouble those children could have gotten into."

"I know. I was a pretty wild kid myself."

That was definitely something she could believe. "You. Wild. Amazing."

"Me. Now, what are you going to do about Wendell? He's your big problem."

"Shoot him?"

"Want some help?"

"Nope. I want to do it all by myself."

"Seriously."

"Seriously, I'll go to court to stop his visitation rights and if he shows up I'm going to pepper his butt with buckshot."

Christian laughed again. "That's my girl. Seriously, do you want me to deliver the court papers?"

"Maybe so. Would you scare him? *Really* scare him, I mean?"

"Sure."

Before Lolly could explore the subject further, her cell phone rang and then Christian's phone chirped.

"Uh-oh. That doesn't sound good." She flipped open the phone. "LaTullipe."

It was her dispatcher. "Chief, they found another body. Sheriff's doing this one 'cause they found him out near the fishing pier in Nueces Pass."

"Okay. Tell him Lieutenant Delacroix and I'll be there in fifteen minutes." She closed the phone.

"Guess you heard." Lolly nodded at his phone.

"Yep, that was C.J. Do you know where this place is?"

"It's about six blocks down the street. I guess we'd better go, huh?"

Christian nuzzled her neck. "I guess so."

He took the partially melted milkshakes and tossed them in the trash can. "I'll treat you again—soon."

THE SCENARIO WAS so familiar it made Lolly want to up-chuck—yellow crime tape, police cruisers, technicians and a black body bag. Olivia was already on the scene talking to C.J. and the sheriff.

"Hi, guys. Anything new with this one?" Lolly asked.

The sheriff had attended the previous crime scenes, so his input was invaluable.

"His driver's license says his name is Timmy Schmidt." The sheriff picked up the plastic ID. "Lives in Houston."

"The good news is we may have a witness." He pointed at an elderly man in hip waders near the ambulance. "I sent him over to the EMTs in case he has a heart attack."

"What did he see?" Christian had parked the car and joined the group.

"He said he was out surf-fishing right before dawn, when he heard a boat out beyond the pier. Then about forty-five minutes later, he snagged the guy with his line."

"Yes!" Lolly exclaimed.

"That's the good news. The bad news is he's almost eighty and doesn't have very good eyesight."

Her optimism deflated.

"But he said it was a fishing boat."

"Commercial or sport fishing?" Lolly asked. It would help to narrow it down that much.

"Commercial." The sheriff turned toward the man who was now sitting on the running board of the ambulance. "But I don't know how much we can rely on his accuracy."

Lolly rubbed the furrow between her eyebrows. "It's the only thing we have."

Christian joined the conversation. "That and the fact that it's been ten days since our last known disappearance. Ten days seems to be the magic number with these guys. How far have you gotten on places with freezers large enough to store a body?"

Lolly leaned against the cruiser and opened her

purse. It was time for an aspirin. "We checked all the restaurants and the packinghouse, but I think they're too public. We need to look at the fishing fleet."

The sheriff pushed back his Stetson. "My men have already checked the commercial sites at the marina, at least the ones here at our pier. But people with smaller boats also ice down their catch." He looked at Lolly and Christian. "Maybe we're thinking too big."

"You might be right," Lolly said. There had to be *something* she'd missed. But what was it?

Chapter Sixteen

Lolly was lurking by her front door when Joe dropped Bren off after his day of manual labor. The kid was so filthy and dejected it almost broke her heart. But he had to learn he couldn't get by with underage drinking and lying. Too much was at stake.

She opened the screen door as he reached the steps and before she knew what had happened, her six-foot-tall son was in her arms. It was a step back in time to when he was a little kid and wanted to be cuddled….

"Oh, Mom, I'm so sorry." Tears made tracks in the dirt on his cheeks. "I know I was wrong. I don't know why we did it." He hung his head. "I deserve to dig ditches all summer. In fact, I probably deserve to do it for the rest of the year."

"You won't be doing it all summer, I promise," Lolly crooned. "Come on." She led him into the kitchen. "Let's have a Coke. It'll make you feel better." And a good talk would make her feel better, too.

She put his drink on the table. "All I want to know is how your dad's involved in this."

Bren gulped down half his Coke. "There was a bunch of us at the Dairy Queen when he drove up. We got to talking about things…and it kind of went from there."

"What things?"

Bren stared at the table, blushing. "Things like how strict you are." He looked up. "Mom, I don't really think you're strict. But I felt I had to go along with whatever he said. Anyway, he offered to buy us some beer and let us have the beach house. Everyone else wanted to do it, so I said okay."

It was just about what Lolly had expected. "I'm going to take some temporary legal action to keep your dad away. If he behaves, we'll figure out some way for you to see him. But if you want to be around him, Mee Maw will have to go with you. I don't trust Wendell."

"Mee Maw?"

"Mee Maw. She scares Wendell."

He hugged her. "I love you, and I'll admit Mee Maw sometimes scares me."

Spontaneous hugs and kisses from Bren had disappeared around the time he entered puberty, so Lolly felt like they'd reached a new plateau. "And I love you, too."

Where were all those tears coming from?

CHRISTIAN QUIETLY MADE his way through the sand dunes. There were only a few die-hard sun worshippers on the beach and it didn't take long to spot Wendell. Headphones, sunglasses, greasy biceps and a beer cooler—the guy was a walking, talking, breathing advertisement for skin cancer.

"Should I stick a fork in you to see if you're done?" Christian had deliberately tucked his T-shirt in so Wendell could see the holster strapped to his belt.

Wendell flipped up his sunglasses. "Who are you and what do you want?"

Christian laughed and deliberately remained standing. "I'm Lieutenant Delacroix, Texas Department of Public Safety." Christian held out his badge. "Chief LaTullipe and I are colleagues. She asked me to come down here to deliver a message."

Wendell took a beer from the cooler. "Talk, but if you hassle me I'll report you."

Christian took the beer from his hand and popped the top. "I don't hassle. I came by for a beer and to remind you about your court hearing on visitation rights." Technically, he wasn't on duty, so Christian chugged the beer. "I also thought I'd let you know I've been doing some research." He smiled. "Your drug arrests in Nevada are interesting, aren't they? Penny-ante stuff, but still…" Christian threw the can in the trash. "Hope you're not as stupid as you look." He slapped Wendell on the shoulder. "If you have any brains in your head, you'll leave those kids alone."

Chapter Seventeen

Lolly's administrative assistant stuck her head in the office door. "Lieutenant Delacroix, you have a fax."

Darn it, that girl twittered every time she saw Christian, and it was beginning to annoy Lolly. "Thanks, Dora. You can go back to your desk now." Three weeks ago the woman had been terrified of him and now she was at his beck and call. Not that Lolly could blame her—he had a way of growing on a girl.

"It's the autopsy on our latest floater. Nothing new. Same caliber weapon." Christian shook his head. "I'm beginning to think the victims are pressure-washed before they're frozen, but where could someone pull *that* off?"

Now, that was the question of the century. "Let's talk about refrigerated trucks."

"Okay." Christian leaned back in his chair. "They kill 'em in Houston. And freeze the bodies when they transport them. That works, but it doesn't tell us where they're washing them."

"Oh, boy, this is making me crazy," Lolly moaned.

"Yeah. And changing the subject, your mother invited me to dinner at your house tonight." He dropped that conversational bomb before he turned back to his computer.

It took Lolly a few minutes to register the segue. "What?"

"Your mother invited me—"

"I heard that part." Mother was at it again. "My mom is matchmaking. How embarrassing."

Christian strolled over and massaged her shoulders. "Don't worry. Any red-blooded American guy would jump at a chance for a home-cooked meal. In fact, I'm starving." He picked up her ponytail and kissed her neck. "Are you ready to leave?"

"Yeah." They'd better get moving or she was going to jump his bones right there in her office. And wouldn't *that* be the talk of the town. With kids, dogs and nosy relatives, it was almost impossible to have a few private moments.

CHRISTIAN PARKED his pickup behind her Blazer. He took her hand as they walked up the back steps. "Is she a good cook?"

"The best. And she loves to feed people." Lolly blushed. "I'm still embarrassed that she's matchmaking."

Amanda and Harvey were on greeter duty at the back door. "Mee Maw is frying chicken and making peach ice cream. And her friend Mr. Bill is here, too," Amanda informed them.

"Amanda, you remember Lieutenant Delacroix, don't you?"

"Sure, I do. You saw my mom with her face all plastered up in green goo." Out of the mouths of babes. "When I grow up, I'm not going to put goo on my face." She tugged at Christian's T-shirt. "Do you think I'm going to need that goopy stuff?"

Christian studied her face. "Nope, and I'm an expert.

You're definitely not going to need goo." He winked at Lolly. "And neither does your mother."

Amanda giggled and ran off with Harvey racing around her legs.

"Flattery will get you everywhere. Come on in and I'll get you a beer."

Mee Maw was cooking while Bill snapped peas.

"I see she has you working," Lolly commented when Bill stood up.

"Yes, ma'am. I believe in earning my keep." He winked. "And your mother is one fine cook." He set aside the bowl of vegetables to shake hands with Christian. "Bill Hemphill."

"Christian Delacroix."

"Have a seat, guys. Do you want a beer?" Lolly headed to the refrigerator.

"Sure. Something smells great, Mrs. Hamilton. I haven't had any fried chicken since the last time I was home."

Obviously the man knew the way to a Southern mama's heart—compliment her cooking.

"And where is home?" Mee Maw inquired.

"Swamp country of Louisiana. My daddy still goes fishin' down on the bayou every morning."

That tidbit initiated a full-fledged discussion between the two men on the merits of live versus dead bait. Yuck!

Bren had wandered into the kitchen. "You remember Lieutenant Delacroix, don't you, Bren?"

The kid extended his hand. "Sure. Mom, did you know he played football in college?" In his eyes, anyone who stepped onto a college gridiron was a hero.

The fact that Christian was a jock didn't surprise her. "Really, where?"

"Rice University."

Now that was a bit more surprising. He had brains as well as brawn. "Hmm."

"What, hmm?" He patted her on the derriere. "You probably thought I had to take off my shoes to count to twenty."

Bren snorted while Amanda giggled.

"That's it. You kids set the table." Lolly motioned toward the dining room. "And use napkins."

Now if they could get through dinner without her kids and meddling mother unearthing major family skeletons, she'd have it made.

No such luck. Christian had a forkful of mashed potatoes halfway to his mouth when Amanda began the inquisition. "Did you ever catch a serial killer?"

"That's not appropriate dinner-table conversation, Amanda."

"Aw, Mama."

Lolly shook her head. "Lieutenant Delacroix is not a homicide detective, and that's the end of the discussion."

Amanda knew when her mother meant business. She turned to Christian. "Okay, then will you play Monopoly with me after supper?"

"Oh, boy, don't do it," Bren groaned. "She's a Monopoly shark and you're just fresh meat."

Lolly shrugged and grinned. "She's going to be a female Donald Trump when she grows up."

"Okay," Christian conceded. "I'll play if I can have the race car. That's my lucky piece."

"How about you, Mr. Hemphill? It's more fun when you have three, and none of the rest of *these* people will play with me." She waved her hand to encompass her family.

"Sure. But I want the Scottie dog."

"Don't say I didn't warn you." Lolly started clearing the table. "Bren, you help us. And you guys can go set up for the great Monopoly challenge." The big bad cop was about to get his butt kicked by a ten-year-old with the face of an angel.

The game had been going on for almost an hour when Lolly offered Christian a Coke. "What's happening?"

Christian frowned as he looked down at his dwindling pile of Monopoly money. "Every time I go around the board I land on *that*." He indicated Boardwalk and Park Place—a quagmire of hotels. "And if I don't get zapped by those, I get hit over there." He pointed at another impressive stack of real estate on the opposite side of the board. Bill didn't appear to be doing any better.

"I told you. She's ruthless. Why don't you just concede?" Lolly asked.

"Not yet. I still have some money left," Christian replied, so intent on formulating a strategy he didn't even look up.

When Lolly walked out of the family room, Christian was trying to make a deal with Bill to trade some property. The man obviously didn't know when he was licked.

"How's it going in there?" Mee Maw asked as she stowed the last pan in the cabinet.

"The fellows are getting savaged."

Mee Maw smirked. "That's my granddaughter. Everything she knows about Monopoly she learned at my knee."

Lolly was afraid that wasn't all her daughter had learned from her grandmother. Within that senior citizen's body beat the heart of a con woman.

"Let's go see if we can end this." Lolly returned to the family room just in time to see her daughter rake all the money over to her side of the table. A Vegas black-jack dealer couldn't have done it with more panache. She was also in time to hear Amanda invite both men to her Ringa Dinga Pizza Palace party.

"Amanda, I'm sure these gentlemen don't want to drive to Corpus to go to a pizza place with a bunch of kids."

Christian smiled. "Sounds like fun to me. How about you, Bill? You on?"

Bill laughed and nodded. "Why not? I'm only going to do this life once, so I need all the experiences I can get."

"Okay, little lady. Tell us where and when."

Bless their pea-pickin' hearts—the idiots didn't know what they were in for.

THE HIGH-PITCHED SQUEALS coming from the backyard rivaled a Rolling Stones concert. Lolly had managed to keep the Ringa Dinga Pizza excursion to a dozen of Amanda's favorite friends, but twelve ten-year-olds was a daunting prospect. Thank goodness she had almost as many chaperones as kids.

Mee Maw, Bill and Olivia were in the kitchen drink-ing iced tea. The gang was all here—everyone except Christian, and if he had half a brain he'd remain AWOL.

Olivia handed her a glass of tea. "He'll be here in a minute."

"Not if he's smart, he won't. We'll wait another fif-teen minutes and then we have to leave. The sooner we get this started, the sooner it'll be over." Lolly held the frosty glass against her face. "We have twelve kids and four or five adults. How many people can you carry in the Suburban?"

"Six kids and two adults," Olivia answered.

"Since you're alone, I'll give you four of the little darlings. Christian and I can fit six in Aunt Sissy's mini-van and Mother and Bill can take Leslie and Amanda in her car. That'll handle them all, right?"

Olivia nodded but before she could answer, the front doorbell rang. "Would Christian come to the front door?"

"I don't think so." Family and friends all used the back. In fact, hardly anyone bothered to knock. With the number of people running in and out of her house, it sometimes resembled Grand Central Station. "I thought all the kids were here, but maybe it's a stray who doesn't know she's just supposed to march right in."

Lolly opened the door, ready to direct the kid to the backyard. Instead, she encountered a set of very wide shoulders. For a moment she was speechless. When she found her voice she almost wished she hadn't. "What in the world happened to you?"

The man was tall and broad and dark, and sexy enough to be Christian—but the person on her porch was an imposter. Gone were the ponytail, the black T-shirt and the boots—replaced by a military-short hair-cut, shorts, polo shirt and running shoes. Ralph Lauren, eat your heart out!

He leaned against the doorjamb. "You're staring."

That was the understatement of the century. She could barely get past his muscular legs, much less his biceps. She'd seen him naked, but somehow leaving something to the imagination was even more exciting.

"Are you going to let us in?" he asked.

Lolly had been so busy ogling Christian she hadn't noticed C.J. lounging against the front porch rail.

Christian stepped through the door and gave Lolly a short kiss. "I thought I'd bring some reinforcements." He nodded at his friend. "Actually, I needed some moral support."

"That sounds like a good idea," Lolly agreed.

C.J. stopped in front of Olivia and tapped her chin. "Sweetheart, *you're* staring." The kiss he planted on her lips was neither short nor sweet.

When the two emerged from their lip-lock, Lolly grabbed her friend's arm and marched her to the kitchen. "What in the name of heaven was that?"

Olivia touched her lips. "I don't know."

"You be careful. He's a narc cop and you can't trust him as far as you can throw him." She had a lot of room to be talking—she was mixed up with the biggest, baddest narc cop of them all.

"Let's go before I have a nervous hissy. Livy, you take C.J. And don't do anything I'd do." She turned to Mee Maw who was gazing at the new Christian with unabashed interest. "Mother, can you and Bill handle three kids?"

"Certainly. We might be old but we're not dead."

Lolly rolled her eyes. "Great. Okay, let's get this show on the road."

After some seat-switching and jockeying for the best position, the small convoy was on its way in a wake of giggles and squeals.

The noise in the minivan abated when Lolly popped in a DVD. She took advantage of the lull in decibel level to speak to Christian. "You really didn't have to come, you know."

"I wanted to."

"So what's with the new image?"

He ran a hand through his spiked hair. "I didn't want

to scare the little girls, and I was tired of the ponytail. So I decided to get cleaned up."

"You don't look like you'll fit in doing undercover now."

"Oh, you'd be surprised. Dope dealers would sell to Little Bo Peep if she had money in her hand. C.J. with his dimples is an all-American poster boy, and he's just about the best narc cop in the business." Christian laughed. "He lulls the bad guys into believing he's harmless."

"And how about you?"

He leaned over and whispered, "I just scare them."

And he was right about that. He scared the piddle out of her, but for a completely different reason. Just when she had him pegged, he up and did something out of character, like chaperoning a kids' pizza party and ditching the biker image so he wouldn't intimidate some little girls.

She was busy thinking when he spoke.

"I've heard about this Ringa Dinga Pizza Palace, but I've never been there. What should I expect?"

Oh, boy. "Well…it's like a bad marriage between Pizza Hut and Six Flags. Loud music, kids running wild and tons of video games. Not to mention they have carnival rides for the little kids." The look on his face was priceless. It served him right for volunteering.

"Don't worry." She patted his knee. "I'll protect you."

FOLLOWING AN ORGY OF pizza and soft drinks, Lolly produced a basket of quarters. She had enough coins to last an hour, maybe an hour and a half, and even that would stretch her Ringa Dinga tolerance.

Olivia sank down on the picnic bench where Lolly

was keeping an eagle eye on her small charges. "Your mother and Bill are about the cutest couple I've ever seen." She indicated the two senior citizens, who'd managed to find a spot far away from the noise of the video arcade.

"Do you think they have sex?" Olivia asked.

"Livy! Bite your tongue."

"Well, they're holding hands. And when they figure we're not looking, they're playing kissy face."

"Yeeeww." Lolly couldn't even contemplate her mother doing the dirty.

Olivia arched an eyebrow. "Senior citizens *do* have sex."

"Yeeeww."

"And where are the men?"

Lolly turned toward the video arcade, where a group of giggling girls crowded around the machines. "They're over there teaching the kids how to shoot bad guys. Swear to goodness, you put a guy in a video arcade and he's ten years old again. I hope I don't get any irate parents complaining about us corrupting their kids."

"Check out those girls flocking around C.J."

"He has a way with the ladies, doesn't he?" Lolly could tell her friend was fighting her growing attraction to C.J. "So what's the deal between you two?"

"There isn't any deal between us."

"If you say so." Lolly tilted her head and smiled. "Let me rephrase this. What was the deal with the red-hot kiss in my foyer?"

She had known Olivia for years and she'd never seen her blush—but wonder of wonders, the woman turned beet-red.

"Nothing. Absolutely nothing. We have a pattern

going. He asks me out and I turn him down. Then every once in a while he'll catch me unawares at the Dairy Queen or in the frozen food aisle at the Piggly Wiggly and he'll kiss my socks off—and stroll off like he doesn't have a care in the world. It's insane. The man has absolutely no sense of decorum—the Piggly Wiggly for God's sake! Right in front of the rump roasts."

Lolly empathized with the kissing-her-socks-off and driving-her-nuts concepts, except that she and Christian had gone well beyond the kissing part. And what *was* she going to do about that?

Chapter Eighteen

Oh, man, Christian didn't even recognize himself! Two days ago he'd chaperoned a kids' pizza party, and now he was taking Lolly to a Kiwanis dinner. When had he become so domesticated?

He parked the pickup and jumped from the cab to assist Lolly. She was undoubtedly capable of getting out of the truck by herself, but he wanted to see those long legs again. Christian would be a happy man if he could spend the entire evening watching her get into and out of his pickup.

The Chinese restaurant was crowded with the movers and shakers of Port Serenity. "I can't believe you talked me into this," Christian complained as they moved toward their assigned table.

Lolly stopped and put her hands on her hips. "We agreed this was a good idea." She shook a finger in his face. "The more people you meet, the more of a handle you'll have on possible suspects."

"Yeah, okay. Whatever."

"And you know I hate that word."

He tweaked her nose. "But you love this." He whispered a lascivious suggestion in her ear. That blush could get him hot and bothered every time. "Let's sit down while I can still walk," he suggested.

"Let me warn you. The food's horrible, the speech will undoubtedly be dull and some of the stuff they do is juvenile beyond belief. But keep in mind that we're here to circulate."

Circulating wasn't Christian's forte, but he could do it. "What's wrong with the food? I like Chinese."

"The Red Dragon is the only Chinese restaurant in the world that serves meat loaf. Need I say more?"

"Ooh, grim."

"Yeah." But not as grim as the fact that Wendell, Jamison Thompson and Nick Abercrombie were seated at the adjacent table. She did *not* want to deal with the Three Stooges. Not tonight.

Jamison sat back in his chair and did a mock salute. "Hey, Chief. How ya doin'?"

Even from six feet away, the beer fumes almost knocked her down.

"I hope you haven't been driving."

Jamison popped Nick on the shoulder. "Oh, no, ma'am. He's driving." Fortunately he appeared to be sober. Wendell, on the other hand, was three sheets to the wind, but at least he was smart enough to keep his mouth shut.

Lolly faced Jamison and Wendell. "If either of you gets behind the wheel of a car, I'll arrest you. Understand?"

"Yes, ma'am," Jamison muttered.

Nick leaned around his friend's chair. "Don't worry, Chief. I'm the designated driver and I'm perfectly sober."

Oh, what she wouldn't give for a Breathalyzer kit.

Toward the end of a boring speech on the capital improvement plan for the school district, Christian excused himself. He went past the men's room and out the exit to the alley. This call required privacy. "Hey, C.J., meet me behind the Red Dragon. I want you to tail someone."

"Anyone special?"

"Just a hunch. Call me when you get here and I'll come out."

"You got it, boss."

Chapter Nineteen

The pungent combination of cigarette smoke, body odor and stale booze wafted back to a booth in the shadows where C.J. nursed a beer. He had followed the idiots from bar to bar before they landed at the Playtime. It was the only dump in Aransas County featuring nude girls. Whoop-de-do!

So far, they'd only been drinking and ogling strippers. They weren't doing anything illegal, as long as they didn't get rowdy or attempt to drive. Secretly he hoped they'd screw up. C.J. was busy thinking about busting one of them when he spotted a very familiar face. It was Olivia Alvarado, in the flesh, standing just inside the door, trying to adjust her eyes to the gloom.

Before his brain could demand that he cool it, he strolled over and got right in her face. "What do you think you're doing here?"

He didn't give her a chance to answer before he took her arm and guided her to the back of the bar. If those boys got a gander at Olivia it could blow his cover sky-high.

He pushed her none too gently into the booth and followed her in. "You didn't answer me." C.J. cupped her chin. "What are you doing here?"

The dirty look she shot him could have corroded steel. "Maybe I missed something, but I don't remember anyone appointing you my keeper." She tossed her hair. "What would you say if I told you I came here to meet a date?"

"I'd say you were lying." Olivia was class personified, and this wasn't her kind of place.

She shoved at his chest. "Let me out of here before I hurt you." She lunged to make a quick getaway and accidentally clipped his nose in the process.

C.J. grabbed her hands. "That hurt! You broke my nose."

"No, I didn't. It's not even bleeding. And if I did, I could set it for you."

C.J. blotted his face with a tiny cocktail napkin. No blood—but his nose hurt like hell. "Not in a million years, lady. I'm fond of my body just the way it is."

Olivia clenched her fist. He was about to get his arrogant face rearranged. Cretin. Churlish lout. Scumsucking bottom-feeder. Not that it was any of his business, but she'd stopped at the Playtime when she noticed his Jeep in the parking lot.

C.J. muttered something, and a second later his lips were on hers. The kiss that was initially a quick peck rapidly evolved into a *Kiss*—with a capital *K*. The raucous sounds of the bar disappeared and time became irrelevant.

Madre de Dios! She was kissing C.J.!

Right in the middle of the good part, he abruptly drew away. Wait a minute! What in the world was wrong with that man?

"Thank God. He's gone."

Even in her dazed condition, those two words were crystal clear. "What do you mean, he's gone?" she hissed.

C.J. grinned, and his dimples made a surprise appearance. "Wendell was heading this way, so I made sure he didn't recognize you."

That did it! Her blood pressure soared into the stratosphere. "Wendell? You kissed me to keep Wendell from recognizing me? How dare you!" She thumped him on the shoulder. "Let me out of here, *immediately*." She wanted to throttle him. But getting him to move was like dislodging a granite boulder.

He pointed at a group of men across the room. "You can't go yet. They have company and if I'm right, it's pretty interesting company."

Olivia huffed in frustration. "Let me guess. You're following Wendell and his buddies."

"Yep. And see the guy who just sat down with them? I chased him all over Mexico last year." He took a cell phone from his pocket and punched in a number. "You're *not* going to believe this. Their contact is José Guerrero." He listened for a few seconds. "Yeah, call me some backup. I've got Olivia here."

He turned and stared at her. "Now, what do I do about you?"

"I'll get up and exit, that's what you'll do about me."

"Nope. They'll see you. You'll just have to wait here until they leave. Then I'll get you to your car."

Olivia wasn't about to go with him to her car or anywhere else. "Don't you have someone to follow?"

He glanced at his watch. "In about five minutes, half a dozen guys will be in the parking lot ready to follow the whole crew. I'll know where José is going before José knows where he's going." He ran a finger down her cheek. "But you still haven't told me why you're here."

The truth would make her look like an idiot, but so

what? She already felt like the biggest fool in Aransas County. She sighed. "I came in here to find you."

"Me." C.J. poked an index finger at his chest. "You came in here to find *me?*"

"Yeah."

The double dimples that had probably seduced a cast of thousands deepened. "Yowser!"

Chapter Twenty

Christian knocked on Lolly's back door. "Are the kids home?" He was sporting a cocky grin.

"Nope. Amanda's at camp and Bren went to Jason's for the day. Why? Do you have something sexy in mind?"

He answered that question by giving her a long, luscious kiss. "What do you think?"

She thought she'd better play hostess or they'd wind up on the kitchen table, a possibility that escalated when he released the top button of her shirt and kissed his way south.

"Wait, wait!" She was breathless. "What if my mother walks in?"

His grin was pure deviltry. "She'll have something to share with Bill."

"Oh, please."

Christian reluctantly buttoned her blouse. "How about a little business first?"

"Hmm." Definitely not as good as the previous idea, but a lot safer.

"We picked up a guy named José Guerrero, who spent a good part of last evening with Wendell and crew."

Lolly put two glasses of iced tea on the table and sat down. "Really? What did he say?"

"He denied knowing anything about the Houston murders. He claims Wendell and his friends are just some nerds who were buying the drinks. But the interesting part is that he says there's someone in town who knows what's goin' down. He also says he doesn't know who it is."

"Do you believe him?"

Christian gave a halfhearted shrug. "Yeah, I believe him. But I sure wanted Wendell to be guilty of something."

Lolly dipped into the freezer for a bag of Oreos she kept for chocolate emergencies. "Cookie?" Lolly offered him one before she crammed a frozen morsel in her mouth.

He shook his head. "Has he tried to contact Bren or Amanda again?"

"No, thank goodness."

"Another interesting thing. Good old José told us some high roller from Colombia is going to be in Houston in a couple of days." He urged her onto his lap. "You want in on the action?"

Lolly nuzzled his neck. "Depends on what kind of action we're discussin'." Heaven help her, she was beginning to sound like a tart.

Christian howled. "Actually, I was thinking of some undercover *cop* work, but if you have something else in mind, I'm game."

JUST BECAUSE a girl was blond didn't mean she was a bimbo. Lolly hated that stereotype, always had and always would. But Christian was right—people told her things they wouldn't tell their best friends. The dolts probably even believed the dumb-blonde jokes.

She'd agreed to the undercover gig, but what in the world could she wear? Her wardrobe wasn't exactly Rio Carnival caliber, and she wasn't about to spend good money on a sexy little nothing she'd never wear again. No, siree—but Olivia probably had the perfect outfit. Every once in a while, that girl liked to get splashy.

The vet clinic was a free-for-all of dogs, cats, puppies and kittens, all waiting impatiently for their turn with the doc. Lolly felt bad about butting into line, but it couldn't be avoided. "Would you please tell Dr. Olivia that the police chief has to talk to her right away? It's an emergency."

The receptionist's eyes were the size of dinner plates as she grabbed the phone.

Olivia flew into the waiting room. "What's wrong? Is it the kids?"

Lolly steered her behind a large potted plant. "Nothing like that. I'm having a wardrobe crisis."

"What!" Olivia squealed and then lowered her voice. "You scared me out of a dozen years, and all you want to do is to borrow an outfit!"

When she put it that way, it did sound stupid. "Hey, look, I'm sorry. I'll ask someone else."

Olivia dragged her through the back exit to the alley. "No way! Tell me what you need."

"Christian and I are heading off to a Latin nightclub in Houston, so it has to be sexy."

"Sexy?" Olivia raised an eyebrow.

"It's not personal! This is for undercover work."

"Undercover?"

Lolly frowned. "Stuff a sock in it and tell me what you have."

"Right now, I've got to see a bunch of cats, a

rottweiler and a poodle. Give me two hours and I'll meet you at my house." She eyed Lolly and giggled. "I have the *perfect* thing."

The giggle should have been a dead giveaway. Two hours later, Lolly was wiggling into the shortest, lowest, tightest silver sequined little scrap of material ever designed by man.

"No way! I look like a hooker." Lolly attempted to pull the dress down her thighs. When she pulled one way, Olivia pulled in the opposite direction.

"No, you don't." Olivia swatted her hands. "You're incredibly sexy. The silver is soooo…" She waved her fingers in the air. "And I have some wonderful shoes." She dug in her closet until she found a pair of strappy sandals. "No hose. And I also have the perfect jewelry." She held up a pair of iridescent crystal bangles. "Fantastic. Christian is going to swallow his tongue."

He just about did, but not for the reasons Olivia had predicted.

"You are not going out in that…that thing." His dark scowl was almost combustible as Lolly paraded into her living room.

Too bad! There wasn't a man in the world who was allowed to tell Lolly LaTullipe what she could or couldn't wear. "I'm wearing this or I'm not going." She did a pirouette with the evil intent of making him crazy. "And if I don't go to Houston, I'm heading over to Cotton-Eyed Joe's." Not that she'd actually appear anywhere in a dress that revealing—except for an official undercover assignment.

Christian made a strangling noise. "I hope I don't have to shoot someone."

He reached over to pull up the bodice, but Lolly

smacked his hand, smiling sweetly as she sashayed out the front door.

Christian glanced at Harvey asleep on the cool hardwood floor. "Harv, my boy, you're lucky you're fixed."

THE BEAT OF Latin music could be felt all the way out to the sidewalk. Christian's gut told him this was a very bad idea. How could the woman look so sexy and be so down-in-her-soul innocent? She had to be oblivious to the impact she'd make. He only hoped she didn't start a riot.

The weight of the gun against the small of his back provided minimal comfort. As far as he could tell—and he *could* tell—she obviously wasn't armed. Oh, man, this was going to be a long night.

MAYBE CHRISTIAN WAS right—the dress was too much, or not enough as the case might be. Every testosterone-packing human from eighteen to seventy-eight was leering. And the way Christian was crowding her she was beginning to feel claustrophobic.

"Can't you pull that up?" he demanded.

Oh, boy, it was time to teach the guy a lesson. "Ohhh-kay." She jerked on the bodice and the hem rode up. Uh-oh!

At that point his eyes almost bulged out of his head. "Pull it down!"

"Make up your mind. You're making a scene. I'm supposed to be sexy and you're *not* supposed to be impressed." She did a Marilyn Monroe moue. "I'm window dressing. Remember?"

He drew her even closer, and she found it hard to breathe. She poked him in the ribs. "Let go of me. People are staring." They were, especially the ladies. And no wonder! He was sexy as all get-out in his black silk shirt and matching black linen suit. But he *was* acting like a jackass.

"Are you armed?" he muttered.

"Certainly. You don't think I'd go into an operation without a weapon, do you?" She smiled and did the pouty thing with her mouth again.

No doubt about it—the woman was trying to drive him crazy. And succeeding! He grunted and let the maître d' lead them to a table next to the dance floor. "My contact said he'd be here later in the evening, so until then we have to act like we're having a good time."

Lolly ran her hands up the front of his silk shirt. "Oh, lover," she said huskily, "I could party with you all night."

Whew! It didn't take a great leap of the imagination from that to fantasies of rumpled sheets. Especially the way her enticing curves were displayed. But every jerk in the joint was also feasting on the sight.

It fleetingly occurred to Christian to cover her with the tablecloth, but he knew how well *that* would be received. Man, oh, man!

Lolly was getting a kick out of the bimbo routine. Every time she puckered up, Christian looked like he'd swallowed a bucket of worms. And when she showed off her attributes, she thought she'd have to practice her CPR.

Lolly was pondering other ways to create apoplexy when the waitress arrived to take their order.

"Glenlivet on the rocks, a bottle of Evian and a California Chardonnay for the lady." Christian played the macho role perfectly.

Well, if that didn't frost her—she was perfectly capable of ordering her own drink. "Hmph!"

"Hmph, what?"

"Just hmph. Brief me again."

"Sometime tonight, my informant, Otis, will show up and ask you to dance. He'll give you the information we need." Christian gave a faint nod at a loud group in the corner. "I suspect our guy is over there, but I need a name."

Lolly refreshed her lipstick, a subterfuge to check out their suspects in the mirror. "How does Otis get his information?"

"He's an accountant and a world-class dork." Christian laughed without much humor. "His clients trust him because he's one of the invisible people. The bad guys are too stupid to understand those are the people who'll bite them on the butt."

Lolly was scoping out the crowd when the waitress returned with their drinks. Several couples swirled around the dance floor in a tango. "They know how to dance." She held out her hand to Christian. "Let's boogie."

"I don't dance."

"Oh, pooh. You danced with me at Cotton-Eyed Joe's."

"That wasn't dancing. That was necking."

True, it had been more like a slow seduction set to music. Just thinking about it made her mouth water.

He scooted his chair close enough for his thigh to touch her bare leg. Then he bent forward and whispered, "Where *exactly* is that gun you're toting?"

"None of your business. If I need it, I can get to it."

A tall dark-complexioned man stopped at the table. "May I dance with the lovely lady?"

"Nope." Christian slid a possessive arm around Lolly.

The man nodded and walked off, while Christian drew up her hand and kissed the palm.

Possessive guys had never appealed to Lolly, but with this man she was definitely willing to make an exception.

"You *are* going to tell me when it's Otis, aren't you?"

Christian offered her other hand the same treatment. "Oh, you'll know Otis."

During the course of the next hour, several brave souls approached the table and requested a dance. Each was met with a cold shoulder—until a short, bald man strolled up. If the man claimed to be over five feet tall, Lolly would've called him a liar. And not only was he extremely short, his chrome dome reflected the lights of the crystal ball revolving overhead.

"Don't tell me—"

Christian nodded slightly.

The man bowed. "Madame, may I have the honor?" The band was playing a slow melody, the first since they'd entered the club. That was probably why Otis had waited.

"Sure." Lolly adjusted her dress. It didn't take long for her to realize the implications of the size mismatch. She looked over his head and frowned at Christian, who had the unmitigated gall to smile. She'd smile, too, right after she got even.

Lolly tapped the top of her dance partner's shiny pate. "If you're Otis, you'd better give me that information before I have to hurt you."

He gazed up at her dreamily. "Can't blame a guy for trying." He cleared his throat. "The man in the corner is André DeLa Joya," he said briskly. "He's the one with the blue shirt. I hear he's mean as a snake. His old man runs one of the Bogota cartels. They sent him up here to check things out. Rumor has it the other three are his bodyguards." Otis continued the conversation talking to her bosom. "Tell the good lieutenant I haven't been able to get a line on who's whacking those guys." Grinning, he led her back to the table. "Apparently, nobody wants to take responsibility." He kissed her hand. "It was delightful, beautiful lady."

Lolly waited until he'd disappeared into the crowd. "Yuck!" She wiped her hand on her dress.

Christian slid closer and nuzzled her neck. "Did we get the information?"

"Yep. The guy in the blue shirt is the Bogota connection—one André DeLa Joya. The rest of them are his bodyguards. And Otis said to tell you he still hasn't found out anything about the murders." She paused as he took this in. "Now what?"

"I need to find someplace quiet to call my captain. After that we'll stick around and see if we can make a contact. If not, we'll go home."

That had potential. All this sparring and touching and nuzzling had fired up her libido—big-time. His apartment sounded like heaven.

Christian was halfway across the crowded dance floor when André DeLa Joya fell off his chair, writhing and moaning in pain. Lolly hadn't heard any shots, but the goons surrounding him instantly produced some mighty impressive firepower.

Christian had to push his way through the growing crowd to get back to their table. Everyone seemed fascinated by the action in the corner.

"What happened?" he asked Lolly.

"Don't know. All of a sudden, I heard a commotion and looked back there." She waved her hand toward the man on the floor. "Our friend fell out of his chair and the goons whipped out an arsenal—but they ditched the firepower when they saw the security guys."

The nightclub crowd was subdued until the paramedics arrived. They strapped André to a gurney, then rolled him out to the waiting ambulance. As soon as they'd left, the band struck up another Latin beat.

Christian took her elbow. "We'll go out the back way and follow them to the hospital."

"What about them?" She was referring to the bodyguards who had dumped their dates and were on the heels of the retreating paramedics.

Christian didn't answer.

They sprinted down the sidewalk to his car. Lolly buckled herself in and stroked the leather seat of the black Porsche Targa. "By the way, where did you get this?"

He pulled away from the curb. "We took it off a reluctant donor. I hate it. I feel like I'm shoehorned into the stupid thing."

If she had his big body and long legs, she might feel the same way, but it really was megasexy.

Christian downshifted. "They must be taking him to the trauma center."

"You think he's that badly off?" Lolly asked.

"I don't know. But they're heading in that direction and so are we." He took the corner on two wheels. "We're not letting him out of our sight. This smells rotten."

"Yeah, I think so, too," she responded.

The minute Christian wheeled into a no-parking zone, the gurney carrying DeLa Joya disappeared through the double glass doors.

Christian jumped from the car and yelled over his shoulder. "Stay out here and see if anything seems strange."

Lolly discovered that getting out of the car quickly was impossible. In fact, just getting out of it without flashing the world proved to be tricky. When she finally popped to the sidewalk, a black Cadillac Escalade screeched to a stop not fifteen feet away. André's trio of bodyguards leapt out, ready for action.

Christian was almost at the Emergency Room entrance when he glanced back to check on Lolly. That was the type of distraction that could get them both killed. Lolly was a professional police officer. She could take care of herself.

Logic flew right out of his head when he spotted the goons less than fifteen feet from the woman he loved. No telling what those idiots would do if she tried to draw her gun. And where had that "woman he loved" stuff come from?

Somewhere in the back of his mind he heard a car engine rev up. But that detail went on the back burner— until Lolly screamed and ran in his direction. He alternately wondered how she could run in those shoes and why a rusted Chevy Citation, driven by someone in a Ronald Reagan mask, was barreling straight for him.

Fortunately his reflexes were highly tuned. Christian dove into a bush as the Citation roared past and crashed into the double glass doors.

One way or another, this case was going to be the death of him.

"Are you okay?" Lolly stuck her head over the top of the bougainvillea.

Christian extricated himself from the vegetation and brushed off his pants. "Yeah. What happened?"

"Some guy in a Halloween mask smashed into the emergency room and then backed out and gunned it. The boys in the Escalade were right on his tail."

"This gets more and more screwed up. We need to find DeLa Joya."

They searched the hospital from top to bottom but DeLa Joya and the men in the green scrubs had disappeared. Poof—gone into the netherworld. Their only clue was the empty gurney.

EVERYONE REALIZED the drug dealer was dead meat. And what reputable hospital lost a patient—as in vanished, mislaid, gone, kaput? Certainly not one that wanted to stay in business.

Dawn was breaking when Christian and Lolly staggered back to the car. "I have to call C.J."

The call was short and if Christian's crabby mood was any indication, it wasn't good news.

"C.J. was checking out a lead that went absolutely nowhere." He rubbed his head. "Sometimes I feel like we're chasing smoke."

Lolly felt exactly the same way.

Chapter Twenty-One

Lolly laid her head on her desk. She felt like a pile of doggy doo—and that was putting it mildly. She'd only had an hour and a half of sleep before she had to take Amanda to camp and Bren to baseball practice. Sleep deprivation was nothing new, but that was merely the tip of the iceberg. Everyone in the office was in a dither about the call from the DEA. You'd think the devil incarnate had phoned. Fortunately, Christian's captain took care of the fed.

And to top it all off, her mother had strong-armed her into an afternoon picnic at the Twisted Oaks Retirement Community.

"Chief, Dr. Olivia's on the phone." Dora's voice reverberated down the hall.

"Dora. I'm three feet away from you. Do you think I'm hard of hearing?" The rebuke drew a chuckle.

She ignored her assistant and picked up the phone. "Hey, Livy. What's up."

"I wanted to see if I could talk you into going to Daisy's for lunch."

"Oh, not today. I have Lance breathing down my neck for a report and I've got to take Mee Maw to

Twisted Oaks for a picnic. Bill apparently thinks we're part of his family." She paused. "Tell you what. Why don't you go with us?"

"Ooooh, no. I don't think so."

"Please, please, pretty please. I can't watch Bill and my mother making goo-goo eyes at each other without moral support."

There was silence on the other end of the line and then a deep sigh. "Okay, I don't have any patients after four. I'll meet you there."

"Livy, I owe you."

"Yes, ma'am, you sure do."

ANY BUREAUCRAT WHO decreed that senior citizens were on the lower end of the economic ladder hadn't visited the Twisted Oaks Retirement Community. With its red clay tennis courts and lush eighteen-hole golf course, it was more like an upscale resort than a repository for the elderly. Ditto for the Beemers and Mercedes in the parking lot. The menu at the annual summer picnic was more likely to feature pâté de foie gras and Dom Perignon than hot dogs and hamburgers.

Bill had saved Lolly and Olivia a prime spot under an umbrella by the pool. He'd also provided plates of snacks and glasses of expensive bubbly.

Olivia nibbled at a cracker covered with lobster spread. "I don't know why you didn't want to come here. If this is any indication—" she raised her cracker "—dinner is going to be spectacular."

"I know I'm being a brat, but I'm having trouble with this relationship stuff." When she was wrong, she'd willingly admit it.

Olivia sipped her champagne. "Tell Auntie Liv everything. Exactly what relationship stuff are you talking about?"

Lolly nodded at the group of people next to the pool. "That, for one thing." Bill and Marcela were holding hands and giggling like teenagers.

"You don't want your mother to be happy?"

"No. That's not it. I want her to be happy and if Bill makes her happy, that's wonderful." She laughed a bit ruefully. "Can you imagine a new stepfather at my age?"

"And what about Christian?"

Now that was getting closer to the crux of the matter. What *about* Christian? She was fascinated, enamored and totally in lust with the guy. But did she love him? She didn't know whether she was capable of loving *any* man. Not after Wendell.

"Lordy, Liv, I don't know how I feel about Christian. Just seeing him makes my insides go all squishy." She studied the contents of her glass as if it held answers.

"So? What about the *L* word?"

"Do you mean *lust?*"

"No, you ditzy blonde, *love.* Haven't you heard? Love makes the world go round." Good thing they were close enough to indulge in affectionate criticism.

Lolly sighed again. "In my heart, I know I love him," she confessed. "But when my head's involved I get all mixed up. I'm scared of getting serious with a cop. And a narcotics guy." She gave a hopeless shrug. "They leave home and don't come back for weeks. I'd never know where he was or the danger he was in. It would drive me crazy and I'm not going to do it!"

"Has Christian mentioned marriage?"

Lolly grimaced. "Nope. That was a big leap on my part. But he's so good with the kids, and my mother approves of him. Even Harvey loves him. Swear to goodness, the dog about has a fit when the guy walks in."

"So what *will* you do when he asks?"

"*If. If* is the operative word. It's a giant step for me to admit I love Christian, but I don't think I'd survive if something happened to him. And it wouldn't be fair to the kids to let them get attached to a new daddy who might get killed in the line of duty."

"Oh, fiddle! That's the silliest thing I've ever heard you say and when we were kids you said some incredibly stupid things. How long have we been best friends?"

Lolly had the grace to be contrite. "Since we were twelve."

"So do you think I'd mislead you?"

Lolly shook her head.

Olivia punched her friend on the arm. "Do you think you're immune to getting hit by a truck?"

Another shake of the head.

"We might not even make it home from this picnic. Here's a news flash: none of us are gonna make it out of this world alive."

Olivia was right. But the question was whether Lolly should listen to her head or her heart. And to complicate matters, he'd never mentioned the word *love,* either. What a mess!

"What about C.J.?" Turnabout *was* fair play.

Olivia looked more than a little sheepish. "I don't know. We're still doing that kiss-and-run thing. I will admit that he's the first guy since my ex-fiancé who can put me in such a dither."

Lolly grinned. Now, wasn't that interesting. Two big bad narc cops and two muddle-headed females!

Chapter Twenty-Two

It had been almost a week since the debacle at the emergency room in Houston, and sure enough, André DeLa Joya had disappeared off the face of the earth. Now every law enforcement agency around wanted to get in on the action. Even the Texas Rangers were breathing down her neck. Something had to break on this case, or Lolly was going to completely lose control of the situation.

She swatted another mosquito and cursed them and the pesky biting flies nibbling on her arm. Not only was she an insect smorgasbord, she was hot and sweaty, and the camouflage uniform was itchy. This was the second night in a row the task force had hidden out in the sand dunes watching the channel. If the murderers followed their usual MO, they'd drop off a body sometime in the next three or four days. Thus, the reception committee. Lolly terminated another mosquito, swearing under her breath.

The radio crackled and Christian's voice came across loud and clear. "Joe's here to relieve you. I'll meet you at the Blazer. I need a ride home."

That was all he would get. Lolly had been avoiding him since her discussion with Olivia. Her behavior was childish, but she needed some solo time.

The Kevlar vest was the first thing to come off. Wearing it was like being baked alive. She had on a pair of shorts and a halter top under her camouflage, so she ditched the uniform, too. Sweat ran down the back of her neck and dribbled between her breasts. Not exactly a sight to inspire anyone's libido.

Christian strolled up to the Blazer carrying his vest. "Hey, cutie, let's go over to the island and do some skinny-dipping." Before she could answer, he stripped off his shirt. If anything could stop a negative response, it was the sight of that man's chest.

"Okay, I'll go swimming. But not skinny-dipping. I'd have to arrest us."

Christian laughed and dug around in a duffel bag until he found a clean T-shirt. "You don't want to get naked with me?" He clutched at his heart. "My feelings are hurt." Before he jumped into the passenger seat, he placed a loud smacking kiss right on her lips. Oooh! Keeping her distance was going to be impossible.

Lolly drove several miles down the hard-packed sand of the beach, past tents full of tourists and bonfires where kids were contemplating orgies. And speaking of orgies, it *was* a full moon—the perfect time to strip naked and frolic in the surf.

Lolly killed the lights of the Blazer and turned to Christian. "I hate jellyfish and manta rays." She shuddered. "Not to mention I'm allergic to sharks."

The man had the audacity to laugh. "I'll carry you. The creepy-crawlies will get me instead of you."

She tried unsuccessfully to resist the urge to be held in his strong arms. "Okay. But just till we cool off. I need to get some sleep. I have to work in the morning."

He walked around to the driver's side of the SUV and

opened her door. "Sweetheart, we all have to work in the morning. C.J. and I have a meeting with my captain in Corpus Christi. I wish I had something to tell him."

Lolly slid down from the car. "So do I, and—" She was about to finish her sentence, but the words were lost when she looked at Christian.

He had stripped off his T-shirt and was removing his combat boots. Bathed in moonlight and half-naked, he could pass for an ancient warrior. All he needed was a mace and a sword. Heavens above, she was waxing rhapsodically about warriors; next thing she'd be spouting poetry whenever she spied a full moon.

"Come on, beautiful lady." He scooped her up in his arms and waded out into the surf.

"Aren't you going to get rid of those?" She meant his camouflage pants. Not that the sight of him in the green military-style pants riding low on his hips was disconcerting or anything. "You'll drown and take me with you."

Christian set her down and the waves lapped against her legs. "If you insist. I was the one who wanted to get naked in the first place."

"Not naked. Just take off those pants."

Yikes, the man was grinning again. And those silk boxers weren't much of an improvement.

"Do you ever watch old movies?" Christian tugged her down to sit with him in the gentle surf.

That was an odd question. "Yeah, sometimes."

"Do you remember Burt Lancaster?"

The guy was somewhat before her time, but Lolly had a sneaking suspicion where this one was going. "Uh-huh."

All doubts concerning a seduction evaporated when Christian loosened the tie of her halter top.

"Did you ever see *From Here to Eternity?*" He untied the back.

"Mmm." The Gulf breeze cooled her breasts, but it couldn't cool her lustful instincts.

The grin on his face was positively lecherous now. "Remember what they did in the surf?"

Before Lolly knew what was happening, she was prone in the waves, reenacting the classic movie scene. "I'll bet Deborah had more sand in her bathing suit than a kitty litter box when they finished shooting."

Christian nuzzled her neck. "You're an incurable romantic, you know that?" Then he proceeded to show her just how romantic *he* was.

Lolly realized that regardless of the sand, Deborah and Burt had the right idea.

Fur flew in every direction when Christian shook out Harvey's blanket. "Not exactly a feather bed, but it's better than the saw grass." He snapped the fabric again.

"Do you really want to lie down on that? I use it when I take Harvey to the beach." She wrinkled her nose.

Christian took a whiff and grimaced. "I'm a desperate man. My bare bottom won't tolerate the sandpaper routine again." He drew Lolly onto his lap.

Snuggling in the moonlight with the man she loved— could it possibly get better? Yikes! To keep from analyzing that idea, Lolly picked up her sand-encrusted shorts and top. "I have to do some major repairs before I go home." She plucked at her ponytail. "Look at my hair." Between the sand, the salt water, the humidity and the wind, she must look like the Scarecrow from *The Wizard of Oz*.

Christian twirled a curl around his finger. "It is kind of sticking up."

Lolly attempted to smack him but before she could hit her target she ended up in a terribly vulnerable—but oh, so delicious—position beneath him, and it was a long time before she had another cogent thought.

Later, much later, she shook out her clothes. "I have to get home. It's late and I need a shower."

Christian grabbed her hand. "We have to talk."

"About where our missing underwear might wash ashore?"

"Nope. I love you and I think we should start thinking about our future."

Lordy mercy! The man was a surprise a minute. Just when she was sure she had him figured out, he did something like *this*. Of course she loved him—loved him, loved him, loved him. But the big question was whether she could make a commitment to a man in his line of work. And if that wasn't cynical, she didn't know what was. She had a lot of hard thinking to do.

"Well," he said ruefully, "that didn't get the reaction I wanted."

"I'm just…just blown away." Lolly peppered kisses all over his face. "I do love you." Hard as that was to admit to him, it was even harder to admit to herself.

Chapter Twenty-Three

The conference room had that sterile public-service look—gray chairs, gray table, gray walls. It was perfect for the painful meeting Christian was having with Captain Thornton and the drug task force. Collectively, they'd called in all their markers, and they still didn't have squat in the way of information. Killers couldn't be invisible. They always left a trail. Someone had to know something.

The captain dominated the meeting from his seat at the end of the table. "DeLa Joya's body will probably show up sometime in the next couple of days. We have every guy we can spare on surveillance. Now we just sit and wait."

Christian stood up to pour himself a cup of coffee. "We need a replay from the beginning. Who benefits?"

The sighs sounded like deflating balloons. The task force had been bouncing that question around for weeks and still hadn't come up with an answer. The logical assumption was that someone, probably the killers, would step forward to fill the vacuum left by the dead drug moguls. But it hadn't happened. "And do we have anything new on this drug connection to Port Serenity?"

The captain shook his head. "Nope, but considering

the bodies are showing up there, we have to assume the mess in Port Serenity has something to do with our phantom drug dealer or dealers."

"Absolutely," C.J. piped up. "But what?"

That was a question they couldn't answer, so they discussed another pending case. The Port Serenity case was big, but it wasn't their only drug problem. Texas had more than its share of imported and homegrown troublemakers.

The captain steepled his fingers. "I briefed you guys last week on the loonies out in the Davis Mountains near El Paso—the dudes who got their hands on a piece of land and declared a separate nation."

One of the other guys snorted. "Yeah, the Texas Republic. They picked a great place to do it. The only signs of life out there are rattlesnakes and tarantulas."

He ignored that comment. "The DEA and Texas Rangers have been staking them out and it seems they've set up some big meth labs and are funneling the product to Dallas-area high schools. The Rangers and DEA are asking if we want to be in on the party." He singled Christian out. "We're putting a team together and I thought you and C.J. might want to go."

In unison, Christian and C.J. answered in the affirmative. Only the worst of the worst tried to hook teenagers on methamphetamines.

"Good. I'll let you know what's happening." The captain dismissed the team and nodded at Christian. "Lieutenant, could I have a word with you in private."

Christian shot C.J. a look. The captain wasn't the chatty type, so a "private" meeting didn't portend anything positive. He was a great boss, but behind closed doors he could be hell on wheels.

"I've been hearing some rumors about you."

Not a good opening, but Christian figured he could handle gossip. He smiled. "And what kind of rumors might those be?"

"I've heard you're diddling the police chief."

Now *that* made him mad. "Don't talk about her like that! She's a classy lady."

"Don't get your boxers in a twist. I didn't mean to be disrespectful. I just don't want you to get into some situation you can't get out of. I also don't want sex—or anything else—to get in the way of either investigation."

Christian blew out a puff of air. "Nothing will get in the way of these cases, but I might as well tell you. I'm planning to ask her to marry me." That was the first time he'd actually verbalized his intention, and it felt like a weight had been lifted. He was going to get married— if he could talk the bride into it, which wouldn't be an easy task.

The captain clapped him on the back. "Congratulations. It's about time you settled down."

"I haven't asked her yet, so I'd appreciate you keeping this under your hat."

"No problem. But how will you deal with commuting between Houston and Port Serenity?"

"I've been thinking about it a lot. I'd like to get a transfer to the Corpus Christi office. I could commute from there. It's time to leave most of the fieldwork to some of the younger guys."

"Spoken like a guy in love."

"Yeah, you're right," Christian admitted. He *was* a man in love.

Chapter Twenty-Four

Christian relaxed against the doorjamb and watched Lolly work on her computer. She was beautiful, smart and funny, and she sure wasn't Marion the Librarian. But the hell with the librarian fantasy; this was the woman he craved. "Hey, cutie, how about a ride with me?"

Lolly gave him one of her breathtaking smiles. "Depends on where you want to go."

"It's a secret. Just tell Joe you'll be gone for a couple of hours."

Lolly clapped her hands. "You're taking me to the Galleria in Houston, right? I always knew you were a shoppin' kind of dude."

"You'll see." He pulled her up from the chair and engaged her in a long kiss.

When they came up for air, Lolly grinned again. "Well…if you put it that way. Let me clear the decks and I'll be right with you."

As they drove, the flat-as-a-tabletop terrain soon gave way to miles and miles of undulating grasslands, live oaks and herds of grazing cattle in the strip of land between the Gulf Coast and San Antonio. She couldn't imagine what Christian had in mind, but speeding up the interstate toward the Alamo City wasn't on Lolly's daily planner.

Christian was wearing one of his bad-boy smirks. Whoa, mama! "Where in the world are you taking me? This isn't the road to Houston, and I don't have the time to go all the way to San Antonio."

"You'll see. Just hang on for a few more minutes."

Lolly didn't have much of a choice. The only thing between her and civilization was cattle, cattle and more cattle.

"It better *not* be San Antonio."

Christian's only response was a chuckle.

"Not S.A., but we're almost there." To back up his statement he took the next exit.

Three Rivers! "You've got to have a screw loose. We're going to Three Rivers?"

"Yup." He turned toward the business district and whipped into the parking lot of the Dairy Queen.

Lolly was floored. "We drove seventy-five miles to go to a Dairy Queen?"

"Yup." Christian unsnapped his seat belt and leaned over the console to kiss her. "Why don't you stake out the picnic table? I'll go in and get you the biggest chocolate shake in the place."

"It's as hot as Hades out there." She felt a pout coming on. "If we have to do this, let's do it in the air-conditioning."

He chucked her under the chin and bent to unsnap her seat belt. "Not private enough."

Not private enough for *what?* What on God's green earth was he up to? Lolly stalked over to the picnic table. It was so hot you could fry eggs on the sidewalk, but under the shade of an old oak tree with a whisper of a breeze, it was bearable. And she did love the sounds and smells of summer in south Texas—crickets and freshly mowed grass. The man walking toward her wasn't bad, either.

Christian handed her a tall frosty cup. "Here you go. A supersize chocolate shake."

It didn't appear that he was going to 'fess up anytime soon, so she'd just sit back and enjoy the sensory delight of chocolate. Lolly stirred the straw in the thick liquid and hit something solid. What was that? Another swirl, another clunk. Terrific! She was hot and sticky, and now she had a foreign object in her drink. Yeech! Lolly plunged her plastic spoon into the ice cream and came up with a chocolate-covered lump.

"What in the world is this?" The devilish smile should've been a dead giveaway that he was somehow responsible.

It was metal, it was round—and ohmigod, it was a ring! Lolly's heart almost stopped in midbeat. A ring! Ohmigod!

She'd made a strange strangling noise and her cornflower-blue eyes were the size of Frisbees, but she hadn't said no; in fact, she hadn't said anything at all. That was a good sign—right? Christian charged ahead and slipped the slightly sticky diamond onto her finger. She'd either flip out or she'd say yes. He hoped it would be the latter.

Wrong again. She wiped the ring on her T-shirt and held her hand up to look at the diamond. Time for some decisive action, Christian decided. "Come here." He drew her into his arms and stroked her back. Tears dampened his shirt. He prayed they were tears of happiness, but hey, he was just a guy. What did he know?

"I'll take this as a yes," he ventured, trying to sound confident.

His comment was greeted with another strangled noise. Maybe he should lose the optimism.

He kissed her. "Do you love me?" he asked. She nodded. "Will you marry me?" She stared at him. "Will you think about it?" She nodded again. That was all he needed. Come hell or high water, he'd make it happen—beautiful wife, a ready-made family, a goofy dog *and* a picket fence.

Lolly gazed at the stunning diamond. The minute she'd seen the ring, her mind had turned to mush. Even though he'd mentioned the future, she'd assumed she had plenty of time to make a logical decision. But no, he'd hidden a ring in a chocolate milkshake. For that reason, if no other, she should politely decline. But, oh, boy, did she ever love him.

Somehow, some way, they'd work through all the flotsam and jetsam of blended families, the risks of being married to another cop and the stress of commuter relationships. Her heart knew it was the right thing to do—even if her niggling voice had some major reservations.

Chapter Twenty-Five

As usual, business at Daisy's Diner was booming. Dishes clattering, waitresses shouting—it sounded like an ordinary day. It looked like an ordinary day, too, but this day was far from normal.

Lolly stared at the diamond on her finger. The ring meant marriage, commitment and home repairs. It meant sharing toenail clippers, for goodness sake. What happened to her pledge that it would be a cold day in h-e-double toothpicks before she got involved with a heartbreakingly handsome guy who had *danger* tattooed on his rump? And when Olivia saw the new sparkler, that woman would squeal loud enough to wake the dead.

Lolly wiggled her finger as the sun streamed in and bounced off the facets of the diamond, creating prisms of color. Was getting married a good idea? Or was she having a fit of insanity?

Lolly watched Olivia as she made her way through the crowd. It always astonished her that her friend was so gorgeous and didn't seem to know it.

Olivia tossed her purse to the other end of the seat. "Okay, my curiosity's killing me. What's your news?"

Lolly smiled. "Oh, just this." She dropped her hand

on the table. When Olivia noticed the ring she screamed, and conversation in the diner came to a halt.

"My God, Olivia. Shush!" Before supper everyone in town would know Lolly was engaged. But *was* she engaged? She hadn't officially said yes. In fact, she wasn't one hundred percent sure she was going to.

Olivia took her hand. "What did the kids say? I want details! Exacting, excruciating details."

Lolly filled her in on the Dairy Queen proposal and her inability to form a polysyllabic reply. "I felt like such a dunce. All I could do was blubber."

"But you did finally say yes, didn't you?" Olivia pressed.

"Not really, but he slipped this on my finger." She waggled her hand in the air.

"And the kids?"

"They high-fived me. I think in kid jargon that's a supersize yes."

"And Mee Maw?"

Lolly laughed. "She got up on the coffee table and danced a jig. Honest to goodness, the woman is nuts."

"So why didn't you dance a jig and give him a resounding *yes?* You, missy, are a real dunce."

"I know, I know."

"And speak of the devil." Olivia indicated Christian, who was strolling over sporting a big grin.

"Scoot over." He nudged her across the seat and took her hand.

"What do you think?" he asked Olivia.

"I think it's great!"

"So do I," he said and then kissed every finger on Lolly's left hand. "So do I. Have you guys ordered? I'm starving. And what could be better than having lunch with the two most beautiful women in south Texas."

THEY FINISHED lunch and walked out into the heat of the afternoon.

"Lolly." Olivia reached for her arm. "I can't tell you how excited and pleased I am. He's really special. But don't tell him I said that." She nodded at Christian who was several steps behind, talking on his cell phone. "And if you don't haul him to the altar, you're totally insane."

"He *is* special. And speaking of special, how's C.J.?"

"C.J. is C.J. He still makes me crazy. But I've had him over for dinner twice in the past week."

"Really? Are you—?" Lolly started a sentence but before she could finish, her phone rang. Two seconds later she heard Christian's cell chirp.

"Not good." Christian flipped open the phone.

No kidding!

"Oops." Olivia's phone rang, too.

Lolly stepped toward the end of the car so she could concentrate on the phone call. From her caller ID she knew it was Sergeant Joe, and that wasn't a good sign.

"Chief, the dude from Houston has shown up and he's a little worse for the wear."

Lolly repressed a sigh. "Where and when?"

"Out at Pelican Cay. He floated up next to a million-dollar house. I'm surprised you didn't hear the screech all the way to town." He chuckled. "Some sea life had used him as fast food."

Pelican Cay was an upscale waterfront development featuring pastel villas, fifty-foot yachts and sleek German automobiles. Those folks lived a good life of gated seclusion and wouldn't appreciate a nibbled-on corpse in their backyard. Thank goodness, Pelican Cay was in the sheriff's jurisdiction.

"I'll be there in a few minutes." She hit the end button and turned to Christian. "Guess you heard."

"Yep. They obviously knew we were watching the beach and went north." He slapped the palm of his hand against his thigh. "How are they getting their information?"

Lolly shook her head. That was the question of the century. She'd bet her house she didn't have a leak in her department, but she couldn't vouch for all the other law enforcement people who'd invaded her territory.

When was this going to end? The simple answer was not till they caught the bad guys—easier said than done.

Chapter Twenty-Six

Lolly was mentally and physically exhausted after the visit to the Pelican Cay crime scene. Thank goodness for mothers who loved to cook. Otherwise, it would've been fish-and-chips night again.

The scene was like something out of *Leave It To Beaver*. Except in this case the cook was Mee Maw, not Mrs. Cleaver, and instead of a shirtwaist and pearls she had on her favorite pair of hot-pink spandex shorts. Christian and Bill were having a beer, and Harvey was stationed under the table waiting for scraps.

From the squeals outside, it was apparent that Amanda and her friends were in the tree house. Bren was the only one unaccounted for.

"Mom, where did you say Bren went?"

Her mother stopped stirring the taco meat. "Bill, Bren said he was going to Jason's house, didn't he?"

Bill took a sip before he answered. "Yep, it was Jason or Josh or Jeremy. I'm not really sure."

"Will he be home for dinner?" Lolly's maternal antenna was on high alert.

"I think so," Mee Maw answered.

"I'll phone Jason's to see when he's coming home."

Several calls later, Lolly's intuition was confirmed. Not only wasn't the kid at Jason's house, he wasn't at Josh's, Seth's, Jeremy's or any of the half-dozen kids she called.

Christian slid his arm around her waist. "I'm sure he's fine."

"He's not going to be when he bothers to come home."

Everyone jumped when the front door slammed. Two seconds later, Bren sauntered into the kitchen.

"Uh-oh." Bill pulled Mee Maw toward the front door. "Let's go out and sit on the swing for a spell."

Christian stood to leave, but Lolly put her hand on his arm. She waited until the seniors had left and pinned Bren with her best "you're in deep doo-doo" stare. "Where have you been? And don't tell me you were at Josh's, Jason's, Seth's or Sean's. I want the truth."

In a nanosecond Bren's facial expression went from fearful to petulant. "I've been with my dad." His chin jutted out defiantly. "He's fun. He said he wants to take me to the Texas Extreme Wrestling Blowout, but he can't tonight because he's got business there." Bren graced her with his patented teenage glare. "I know you won't let me go. You never let me do anything fun."

"Sit!"

She was surprised when he acquiesced. Heaven help her. Every kid from thirteen to eighteen should be hauled off to a desert island until adulthood.

"Bren, Bren, Bren." Lolly hugged his stiff body. "If you want to see your father that badly, I'll work something out with him. But I want your word that if anything he ever says or does makes you uncomfortable, you'll call me. Promise?"

Bren shied away. "Yeah." He sidled past her and disappeared down the hall.

Christian crooked his finger. "Come here." When she did, he pulled her into his lap.

"I'm not a kid expert, but I do remember being a teenager. Don't take it personally. It's what they do." He kissed her nose. "Okay?"

She sniffed. "Okay."

"That's my girl." He pushed a curl behind her ear. "But he did say something that caught my interest."

"What?"

"Wendell has a business meeting at the wrestling match." Christian smiled. "Now what kind of business associates do you think he'd be meeting at the TEWB?"

"Drugs?"

"Possibly. Maybe Wendell's into something illegal. He has a record, and a couple of his friends aren't exactly pillars of the community." He gave her a long, slow kiss. "Do you feel like getting big-haired and slutty so we can check out your scumbag ex?"

Lolly thought about it for a few seconds. It might be bad karma, but she was desperate to pin something, anything, on Wendell. "Okay, I think Mee Maw can spend the night. She said Bill was going fishing. But I draw the line at slutty."

Christian ran his hands up under her T-shirt. "You don't have to be slutty to be sexy."

"Do I get a treat tonight?"

"Oh, yeah. You're definitely in for a treat."

THE COLISEUM PARKING LOT was a sea of pickup trucks sporting rifle racks. But what had she expected? These were the same folks who flocked to tractor pulls. Tight jeans and big hair were the norm.

Lolly adjusted her ponytail. She didn't have a bushel

basket of hair, but she wore enough blue eye shadow to make Bozo the Clown jealous.

"I feel ridiculous."

Christian grinned.

"Okay, considering everyone else—" she waved her hands at the crowd milling toward the arena "—I'm downright conservative."

"Uh-huh." Christian walked around to her side of the pickup. "Come on, princess, time to catch the Hunka Hunka Burning Love."

Normally she wouldn't mind missing the Hunka Burning Love, Ivan Botski *and* Silk Stockings. But tonight, she was a wrestlin' kind of babe.

Christian led her into the Coliseum. "We have seats near the front."

Hard-rock music blared from the overhead speakers as strobe lights skittered in a random pattern over the audience.

"Couldn't we sit farther back, where it's quieter?"

Christian either couldn't hear her or chose to ignore her.

"Are all these people on speed?" They were waving handmade signs and hooting at the top of their lungs.

He put an arm around her shoulders. "Hang on to my belt loop and we'll find our seats."

Lolly followed him down the crowded steps. They were close enough to see sweat dripping off the announcer's face.

"Do you think C.J.'s here yet?"

Before he could answer, Christian's phone rang. He talked for a few minutes and snapped the cell closed. "He's here. I hope this isn't a wild-goose chase."

The house lights dimmed as colored floodlights flashed and the music grew to a deafening crescendo.

It looked and felt like a cross between a Grateful Dead gig and an Alabama concert.

"Oh, my gosh, look at that." Lolly indicated the Hunka Burning Love's ugly mug featured on a multi-story screen. The sound level in the Coliseum tripled when the Hunk strutted down an adjacent runway swearing and delighting the crowd with an exuberant one-fingered salute.

"Unbelievable," Lolly muttered.

"You ain't seen nothin' yet. Take a gander." He motioned toward a ramp at the other end of the ring.

She looked—and saw a partially clad Amazon being carried into the arena on a bejeweled litter by six muscular men. Scary!

"Her stage name is Dee Dee of the Desert," Christian said. "That's what all the veils are about."

Lolly shifted in her seat to see him better. "And how do you know all this?" She took another look at Dee Dee, who was strutting around in a pair of stiletto heels. When she waved her veils at the Hunk, the crowd went bananas.

"Swear to goodness!"

Christian squeezed her hand. "*They* seem to like her."

Lolly surveyed the audience. Sure enough—glazed eyes, drool, the whole enchilada.

"Don't tell me she's going to wrestle *him.* She's a big girl, but he outweighs her by at least a hundred pounds."

"Nope. They have tag-team partners. Watch the screen. In a few minutes the other two will show up."

She punched him on the arm. "How *do* you know this stuff?"

"I looked on the billboard while you were ogling the people."

Yep. The audience was almost as fascinating as the farce going on in the ring. "Okay, smarty pants, who's coming in next?"

He glanced at the balcony. "Look up there."

"Oh, my word!" A voluptuous blonde in silver lamé with wings and landing lights sailed over the heads of the audience. It was all silliness and pageantry—the ultimate theatre.

Christian laughed at her reaction and kissed her hand. Then his cell phone rang.

"Yeah. Okay. I've got it. Keep your eye on him." He closed the phone. "Wendell and Nick are two sections over, thirteen rows up from ringside." He took out a pair of small binoculars and scanned the crowd. "Got 'em." He handed the glasses to Lolly. "Over there." He motioned at a section of the crowd on his right. "C.J. is covering Abercrombie and I'm taking Wendell. Keep the ball cap on." He had insisted she put her hair up and wear a cap as a disguise, however lame.

"Wendell's on the phone." Christian homed in on their quarry. "Okay, guy, now go, so we can follow you," he muttered. "Yeah, that's it. Let's hope we get some action." He hit Redial on his cell phone. "He's finally up and moving," he told C.J. "You keep an eye on the other one." Christian nodded a couple of times and hung up.

"Stay here. We can't have them recognizing you."

Lolly reluctantly agreed. It galled her that she couldn't be in on the action, but he was right. She pulled down the brim of her hat and waited. Oh, boy, she hated waiting.

THE HALL OUTSIDE the arena was vacant, except for the people at the hot dog stand.

Wendell appeared to have a specific destination in mind; he didn't tarry by the vendors or head into any of the numerous restrooms they passed.

In many ways, the cell phone had made law enforcement's job a whole lot easier. But it also allowed the bad guys immediate access to trouble.

"What's our other friend doing?" Christian asked when C.J. answered the phone.

"Abercrombie's your friend?" C.J. repeated with a snicker.

"Stuff a sock in it. What's happening?" he growled.

"Buying a beer."

Christian watched his prey, who was moving closer and closer to the rear service entrance. "Okay, get someone to tail Nick, and you and a couple of guys head toward the back. I'm afraid Wendell's about to leave."

"Okay, boss. Watch your back."

"Always do."

Christian lost sight of Wendell as he rounded a corner. Although it would be easier to follow the guy in a crowd, this was still a cakewalk compared to some of his other surveillance experiences. He'd give fifty bucks for a crowd of mouthy teenagers, but the only other person in the hall was an elderly Asian man.

In the distance, Christian saw an exit sign and the boy/girl indicators for the restrooms. Wendell could be doing anything or nothing at all. Whatever he was up to, Christian was going to stick to him like glue.

He stepped into a dimly lit alcove as his prey made a sharp turn into the bathroom. The guy was obviously meeting someone. Time to call in the troops. No telling who they might snare. Christian was about to call C.J. when he was stopped by a feeble voice.

"Sir, sir. Would you help me?"

The Asian man had collapsed against the wall clutching his chest.

Bloody fantastic! This old guy was going to screw up the whole operation.

Christian approached the stricken man. "Are you having a heart attack?" The man fell against him, one hand grabbing Christian's shirt. "I'll call 9-1-1." Christian reached for his phone but stopped when he felt something hard pressed against his gut. Not good—the old guy had the drop on him. Christian was bigger, stronger and younger—and the most gullible dolt in town.

"Don't even consider it, Lieutenant. You wouldn't be the first man I've killed." Apparently the heart attack *victim* had miraculously recovered. Christian was in a boatload of trouble.

"Just in case you have any buddies watching, put your arm around me like you're helping me. We're going in there." He indicated the restroom. "Hand me your gun with your left hand." Christian complied. "Now give me your second gun and your handcuffs."

Christian felt like the biggest jerk on the face of the earth. The guy was seventy if he was a day. Damn, he'd get laughed off the squad—if he managed to live that long.

"Let's go, and make it convincing."

After they'd stepped into the bathroom, another man blocked the door with a cleaning cart.

What the— Bill, Mee Maw's Bill, was holding a silenced 9-millimeter to Wendell's head.

"Christian, I'm really sorry you got involved." Bill shrugged his shoulder at Wendell. "We were going to scare this skunk out of a couple of decades of life. Then maybe he'd straighten up and leave the good people alone." He yelled over his shoulder. "Carl, get out here. We have a problem."

Christian recognized Carl from a visit to Lolly's house. What was happening? These guys were old, but apparently they weren't too old to be toting guns. And judging by the efficiency of their operation, he was beginning to realize they weren't too old or incapacitated to participate in felony kidnapping. Had they been involved in an even more heinous activity?

"Lieutenant, raise your hands, please. Minh, please step away from him. He's fast and smart, and I don't want to hurt him. But I'm not going to jail. I'm too old for that."

Christian did as he was told. If he could stall long enough, C.J. and the troops would arrive.

Bill smiled. "I know you have someone else coming, so we'll make this short and sweet." He turned to Wendell, who'd gone a bilious shade of green. "You're one lucky schmuck. From now on, leave the kids alone." Wendell fell like a rock when Carl hit him.

"That idiot thought he was going to do a drug deal. Guess we fooled him, huh?"

Bill scooted Wendell's prone body out of the way. "And Lieutenant, just to satisfy your curiosity, we're the guys you've been looking for. Ironic, huh? Just goes to prove that old folks are invisible."

These geezers had gotten the drop on some of the toughest drug dealers in the drug world—amazing. But what was their motivation? "I hate to ask this, but why?"

"It started very innocently. We were sitting around playing poker and arguing about the afterlife. Then we started wondering how we'd stack up when we got to the pearly gates." Bill grinned at his compatriots in crime. "Since we'd all been involved in some felonious activities, we didn't figure we'd do too well with St. Peter. And frankly that scared the hell out of me—so to speak."

The other men nodded as Bill continued. "The three of us, along with a couple of other guys, had a very lucrative business running drugs out of the Golden Triangle during the Vietnam War. It was a wild time. We smuggled heroin in body bags, on cargo pallets, in just about anything and everything you could find. Bill was flying for Air America, and I had the CIA contacts. Blinky knew all the high Vietnamese muckety-mucks. And we had some load masters on our team."

Bill shrugged, raising both palms. "At the time, we didn't think about the lives we were ruining. And now that we're getting to the end of the party, we're feeling bad about all the misery we probably caused."

Carl nodded and continued the explanation. "We were so freaked out by the idea of going eyeball-to-eyeball with the devil, we decided to put some marks in the plus column."

Bill jumped into the conversation again. "So in our own unique way of seeking redemption, we decided to help out the good guys, people like you." Bill pointed at Christian. "And to do that, we get rid of the drug-dealing scum. The difference is, we were gentlemen. They're just thugs."

Unbelievable! There was no way Christian could have imagined something this off the wall.

"Minh, please tie that one up." Bill gestured contemptuously at Wendell. The elderly Asian produced a roll of duct tape and trussed Wendell up like a Thanksgiving turkey.

Bill turned to Christian next. "I'm sorry to do this to you because I respect you." He motioned Carl and Minh back. "Lieutenant, please be good enough to sit and face the sink."

Christian didn't have much of a choice, so he sank onto the floor.

"Blinky is going to handcuff you to the pipe. Please don't give him any trouble."

Sighing, Christian stuck his hands out.

"And Carl's going to tape your feet and mouth. We need a few minutes to make a getaway. If you search my place at Twisted Oaks, you'll find everything else you need. You just won't find us."

Bill tossed Christian's cell phone into the corner. "You're resourceful. You'll figure out how to retrieve that. I'm sorry I won't be around for your wedding." Then the three elderly men strolled out the door.

The silence was worse than having a gun to his head. Christian braced his feet on the wall behind the sink and yanked with all his strength. Pain rocketed to the top of his head. The drain gave slightly when he jerked it again. Third time had to be the charm—and when the pipe gave way he barely missed smashing his head on the floor. He was too old for this!

Christian clawed at the duct tape on his mouth as he crawled over to the phone and hit Redial. C.J. answered before he could get the tape completely off his mouth.

"Yo, boss."

Christian jerked the tape off. "Get a move on! We're in a mess of trouble."

Chapter Twenty-Seven

C.J. and two other officers arrived about the time Christian got the tape off his ankles. His wrists were bleeding, but he felt lucky to be alive. Wendell was unconscious and lying half in and half out of a stall.

Christian explained the situation to C.J. Then he called the DPS dispatcher to get an APB out on the suspects.

LOLLY WAS CHEWING on a fingernail and almost jumped out of the seat when her cell phone rang. Christian tersely asked her to meet him at the front door. From the tone of his voice, she knew they had a problem, and when she saw his bloody wrists her suspicions were confirmed.

"What—" Before she could say anything else, Christian steered her through the door and sprinted to the parking lot.

"I'll tell you everything in the truck. We have to get back to Port Serenity."

True to his word he filled her in on everything, starting with being suckered by a man half his size and twice his age and ending with Bill's escape. "The DEA boys are headed out to Twisted Oaks and I want to be there."

Lolly threw her baseball cap in the seat behind her. If she released her ponytail, maybe the headache would go away. Yeah, right.

She rubbed the back of her neck. "How in the world did we totally miss this?" On an unbelievability scale of one to ten, this one rated at least a twenty. Her mother was in love with a serial killer. His friends were murderers. The deputy dogs with the radar gun and citizen-cop badges were responsible for the human Popsicles.

"I'd rather be gutted with a rusty oyster shucker than tell my mother that Bill's a killer, even if in his convoluted reasoning he somehow thought he was doing the right thing."

Christian didn't speak as he put the police light on the dash and stomped on the accelerator. They made it home in half the time it normally took.

This was the most exciting thing to hit Port Serenity since the fertilizer plant blew up. A fleet of marked and unmarked police cars, swarms of uniformed and plain-clothes officers and strings of yellow police tape had enticed most of the elderly residents out to the street. Even Oprah couldn't compete with this spectacle. Everyone wanted to be the first to see, the first to know, the first to come up with a good story.

She followed Christian past the string of tape wrapped around the front door of Bill's pink stucco town house. A DEA agent from the multijurisdictional task force was standing in the foyer shaking his head.

"What do we have?" Christian asked.

"Nothing. Absolutely nothing," the man answered.

Lolly hadn't been in Bill's place since the picnic, but she could tell that something was out of place. Then it hit her. The pictures, the knickknacks—everything personal was gone. It was more like an expensive hotel room than a home. Obviously he'd made contingency plans.

Lolly stuck her head in the kitchen, but it appeared to be as sterile and unused as the rest of the house. "Have you guys been to Carl Harper's place?"

"We have a team there right now, but from what they're telling me, it doesn't look like anyone lives there, either."

Christian paced the small foyer as he ran his fingers through his hair. "We have to find them."

The DEA agent nodded at the technician who was fingerprinting the living area.

"We've got a team setting up over at the community center to interview those folks." The DEA guy indicated the crowd assembled outside. "I'm sure one of those people can ID the rest of the men. In fact, I'd bet my pension half the people out there knew what was happening."

Lolly prayed that a couple of people near and dear to her weren't in that loop.

Christian took her elbow and steered her out the door. "Let's go help with the interviews."

"I suspect someone I love has a treasure trove of information," Lolly whispered.

"Yeah. And that's why I think we should be over there. I'd bet my bottom dollar she's going to show up within the next thirty minutes."

The crowd in the community room was almost as large as the group outside. Lolly was busy clipping her badge to the front of her shirt and locating a notebook when a geriatric gnome swathed from head to toe in a flannel nightgown grabbed her arm. "I know some things. Important stuff," she whispered.

No kidding. The woman had probably been on the *Titanic*. And flannel! The heat and humidity in the room were enough to knock over an elephant.

"Yes, ma'am. I'm Chief of Police LaTullipe. Why don't we sit over there and you can tell me everything you know."

Unfortunately, everything the woman knew was gossip, and if even twenty percent of this stuff was true, Viagra truly was a miracle drug.

They had just finished talking when Lolly spied Mee Maw and Aunt Sissy. Lolly had just one prayer. Please God—don't let them be involved. Heaven forbid she'd have to throw the two women she loved most in the pokey.

Lolly hadn't seen her mother that distressed since the day of her dad's funeral. She looked terrible and Aunt Sissy wasn't in any better shape. Lolly hugged the two women.

"Come with me." She led them into the kitchen and shooed everyone else out. "Sit here. I'm going to get Christian." It was probably due to the shock, but Mee Maw followed her instructions without any argument.

Deep down in her professional gut, Lolly realized she should let someone else handle this. But she couldn't, she *wouldn't,* do that. Her mother needed her more than she'd ever needed her, and Lolly wasn't about to let her down.

Christian had apparently seen where they'd gone because he was there before Lolly got to the door. He hugged Mee Maw and then included Aunt Sissy in that hug.

Merciful heavens, she loved that man.

He took Mee Maw's hand. "Do you know anything about this?"

It was obvious from her expression that she did.

"What do you know?" he asked.

"This." She handed him a padded manila envelope. "He said if anything ever happened to give this to you and Lolly. I thought he was just acting crazy, but I hid it someplace safe, and then I forgot about it."

She yanked a wad of tissues from her purse and blew her nose. "When Mrs. McCarthy called me, I grabbed it out of the freezer and brought it with me. That's chocolate ice cream." Mee Maw pointed at a brown smear on the bottom of the envelope.

Most people used a bank for their valuables; her mother relied on the freezer.

Christian unsealed the envelope and a key dropped out—it looked like a key to a bank deposit box or a safe.

Had Bill been considerate enough to leave a confession, a paper trail? Lolly slid her arm around her mother, who was quietly sobbing.

"I can't believe he's gone."

Neither could Lolly. Just when you thought you knew people, they up and sucker punched you.

"I'm going to take Mama and Aunt Sissy to my house. I'll get them settled and come back." She shepherded the two women out the back door and retreated to the sanctuary of home.

When they got there, Bren jumped in to take care of his grandmother and great-aunt. Teenagers could sometimes be a godsend. He was plying them with grilled cheese sandwiches and sweet tea when Lolly hurried back to Twisted Oaks.

Most of the police were gone when she arrived, but Christian was still in Bill's living room poking around.

"Find anything?" She plopped down on the overstuffed couch. The room was covered in fingerprint dust. What did the technicians expect to find? They had the identity of the perpetrators, after all. Still, it might be solid backup for a court case, if they ever found Bill and company. For her money, she'd bet it would be a long time before they surfaced again.

Christian sat down with her. "The safe's concealed in an upstairs closet. They were about to call a locksmith. Good thing I had the key, huh? Turns out Bill kept a journal, a virtual road map."

He took Lolly's hand. "Do you remember Mee Maw saying that he owns an oil-well drilling company? Seems some of his rigs are out in the Gulf. And guess what? Once the oil starts flowing, they keep a two-man crew out there to check the gauges. Those guys change out every two weeks. Seeing a pattern here?"

"Oh, my gosh!"

"And—" he paused "—they have huge freezer units on the platforms."

"Are you kidding?"

"Nope. What do you bet some of the men who work for Bill's drilling company are old buddies from Southeast Asia? What do you bet they were also load masters during the Vietnam War?"

Lolly rolled her eyes. "I hate to even ask."

"Guess who owns a fleet of shrimpers?"

"Well, considering that half the shrimp boats on the Gulf Coast are owned by Vietnamese, I'd say Minh Pham."

"Right," he concurred.

"Does the journal explain anything more than what he told you?"

Christian shrugged lightly. "Yeah, like he said, they thought they were helping us. They figured if they did a dramatic takeout of the bosses, the little cockroaches would scatter and the drug networks would fold. It was their convoluted way of scoring some points with the heavenly honcho. I think they picked Port Serenity—and moved here—because it was convenient and—" Christian laughed at his own joke "—they probably don't drive at night."

"Those devious old goats!" she exclaimed.

He grimaced. "You got that one right."

Chapter Twenty-Eight

It had been almost two weeks since the scene at Twisted Oaks, and things were slowly getting back to normal. Port Serenity's crime had reverted to mailbox smashing and double-parking. Most members of the alphabet soup of law enforcement were long gone. And some old memos had surfaced at the Defense Intelligence Agency that confirmed everything Bill had said. The DIA had suspected the men were running a big-time operation, but couldn't pin anything on them. And then, when Bill's little cottage industry vanished, official interest evaporated. Amazing!

The first week following Bill's disappearance was unbearable. Even though Bren and Amanda did their best to console Mee Maw, it hadn't worked. Lolly tried to help, but she felt powerless. She was ready to have her feisty, outspoken mother back. She was too young to switch roles with her mom—yep, way too young!

Christian was supposed to get back from Houston tonight, and when he did, Lolly's mood was going to improve considerably. The kids both had sleepovers, and the house was all hers. They could make red-hot love on the kitchen table, in the bathtub or even on the washing machine.

Red hot—just like the man standing in the doorway. Skintight jeans, scuffed boots, black T-shirt stretching across his chest and that black-as-night hair rumpled from his motorcycle helmet.

"Hey, beautiful, do you have anything cold to drink? I'm dying of thirst."

So was she, but hers didn't come from a hundred and fifty miles on a "hog."

"Right there." She indicated the refrigerator. A good hostess would pour it for him, but a good hostess wouldn't get a view of a scrumptious butt in tight denim. So let him pour his own drink. She'd just watch, thanks anyway.

When he leaned into the refrigerator Lolly took the opportunity to put her arms around his waist and slide her hands under his shirt.

He chuckled and stopped her roving hand. "I'm sweaty."

"Not as sweaty as you're going to be."

"And hot."

"Oh, I'm counting on it." Was she finally getting good at flirting and verbal foreplay, an art she'd missed out on in junior high?

Before she could consider that question, he had her backed up against the wall, holding her hands up by her face. He alternated nibbling and kissing her neck. Nibbles, kisses, nibbles, kisses. And he wouldn't let go of her hands. It was driving her wild.

"Bed?" she inquired sweetly.

He stopped a trail of kisses halfway down her collarbone and looked up. His smile was the devil's own. "Nope. But we do need to get rid of these." Off went her top; then her shorts disappeared. Of course, the underwear didn't stand a chance.

"Let's see, where was I?" The twinkle in his eye gave him away. The man was up to no good. And thank the good Lord for small favors! He continued with the hot, wet kisses down to her breasts.

His jeans felt rough against her skin, and the light abrasion was indescribably erotic. And as for being naked when your lover was fully clothed—oh, baby, it was incredible.

"WE COULDN'T BE doing this if the kids were home." Lolly took a sip of wine and relaxed against Christian's chest. What two determined people could do in a big, old claw-footed bathtub was pretty impressive.

He took her wineglass and put it on the floor, and then he proceeded to do what he did best.

"We can when we get married. We'll just lock the door." Christian turned her around to face him. "I think we should get married right away."

Right away! By right away, did he mean next week or next month? Either was too soon to pull together a wedding.

"I thought we'd have a really small shindig with just the family, plus Olivia and C.J. Your mom isn't ready for anything more elaborate."

"Before we discuss where and when, we need to talk about some minor details like living arrangements and jobs." She waved her hand in the air. "Little stuff."

Christian kissed her nose. "You're cute when you're flustered. I have it all worked out. I'm transferring to the Corpus office. That way I can commute and we'll live here. And pretty soon I'll be able to get out of the undercover business."

Lolly put her arms around his neck and rubbed her

breasts against his chest. Up and down. Up and down. The soapy friction of skin against skin was heaven.

"That's enough to bring me home early."

"When will your transfer go through?"

"In a couple of weeks. But first C.J. and I are going out to El Paso for a while." He pushed a wet curl behind her ear. She had a bad feeling about this conversation.

"Some folks out there are causing big trouble. They have a few thousand acres of desert and claim they've seceded from the state and the union. According to them, they have the right to make drugs, refuse to pay taxes and wage war with law enforcement. Let's just call this my last hurrah."

Anything she said would be useless. For weeks she'd been practicing her Scarlett routine—thinking about it later. But later was now, and she had to make peace with the fact that the man she loved worked in a very dangerous profession. What made her assume he was immune to a bullet or a knife-wielding junkie?

"So when are you getting back?"

"Three weeks, max."

"So should I reserve the church for the weekend after Labor Day?"

"Oh, yeah." He sealed the bargain with a deep kiss.

Chapter Twenty-Nine

If patience truly was a virtue, Lolly should be considered a saint. She needed to hear from her man. Christian had been in El Paso for almost a week, and in all that time he'd only managed a few short phone calls. Lolly might be a small-town cop, but she knew all about stakeouts—greasy fast food, long uncomfortable hours and boredom. So why didn't he whip out that cell phone and let her know he was okay?

IT HAD BEEN the longest week of Christian's life. He was hunkered out in the sagebrush with a couple of sheriff's deputies who had minimal regard for hygiene, there wasn't a cell tower for miles, and the only line of communication was a satellite phone the bean counters watched constantly. It was like being incommunicado in purgatory.

Task force members had surrounded the headquarters of the Texas Republic, but with thousands of acres it was almost impossible to corral everything and everyone. So the drugs were still leaking out to the big cities. And kids' lives were still being ruined.

The week was finally over and he was ready for a hot

shower, a cold beer and a soft bed. But first, Christian
had to meet with C.J. Leave it to the Beaver to find the
best eatery in town. Checked oilcloth on the tables;
truck drivers and waitresses with big hair—this one had
all the earmarks of a great meal.

Both C.J. and Christian ordered the Guadalajara special, enough food to feed half of west Texas. Christian's
mouth started watering the minute the waitress put the
steaming-hot plate in front of him. He stuck his fork into
a tasty dish of masa, cheese and green chilies. "What
do you know about the sheriff's guys?" he asked.

Christian had a really bad feeling about this operation, and C.J. had been a great sounding board for years.
A couple of the local boys were bumbling idiots; however, they seemed to be following protocol. So what
was wrong?

C.J. chewed thoughtfully. "The folks out here are
pretty independent. But if we have a dirty cop on our
hands, it would explain why the bad guys always know
when we're coming."

"What do you think we should do?" Christian asked.

"Wait and see. What else?"

Christian grimaced. How many times had he heard
that line since he'd been working undercover? *Wait and
see. Wait and see.* It felt like a bad mantra.

"HEY, PRINCESS, how's everything on the home front?"
It went against every rule to call Lolly, but Christian had
to get in touch with someone good and innocent.

"Fine. Bren's going to be the quarterback on the
freshman football team. He's anxious for you to come
home and work out with him."

Those two simple words, *come home,* made his day.

"Amanda and I went shopping for school clothes and I let her buy some hip-huggers. I can't believe my baby's growing up. Next thing she's going to want is a tattoo—and a navel ring."

Christian laughed. "Not quite yet, but give her a couple of years. If we're lucky the fad will be over by then."

"We can hope. Are you okay?"

"Yep." He couldn't tell her anything, not that he actually knew much.

"Olivia and I went to Corpus looking for dresses for the wedding." She giggled—not a sound he'd heard very often from her. The fact that he could make her giggle made him feel good, too. He couldn't believe she'd finally said yes.

He was letting her carry the weight of the conversation. He needed a world that didn't reek of drugs and evil.

"Wendell and I had a long talk."

"Really. What did Wendell have to say?"

There was a pause, and then Lolly decided to share the news, even if it might be premature.

"He has an opportunity to join a band playing the cruise-ship circuit. So he's not going to be around much. Want to know the *really* good news?"

Having Wendell out of the picture was enough to make him hoot and holler. "Sure."

"I got up the courage to ask the big question, and he agreed to let you adopt the kids."

"Yes!" That *was* good news. Christian hoped the kids would be as excited as he was.

"I love you," she whispered.

"I love you, too." He was terrible with words, but in this case all he had to tell her was the simple truth. "I miss you so much I ache. I can't wait to get home."

The conversation was interrupted by an insistent banging. "Someone's at the door. I've got to go. Remember, I love you. I always will. I'll call you again soon."

Christian hung up and stalked to the door. "This better be good."

C.J. ambled in. "Good, I'm not so sure. The sheriff called and said we need to be down at headquarters right away. Said he couldn't get hold of you."

Christian grabbed his holster. "What's up?"

"Don't know. I guess we'll find out soon enough. I'm getting signals from my bad-news vibe."

Unfortunately, Christian knew exactly what he meant.

AERIAL RECONNAISSANCE HAD located a compound of trailer houses doubling as meth labs in a remote canyon. With only one way in and one way out, it resembled the hideout for the old Hole in the Wall gang. With a half-dozen automatic weapons, the perps could hold off a virtual army. A surprise attack was mandatory, or things would get deadly.

The task force had deployed thirty men who were supposed to land in a canyon a couple of miles from the compound. From there they'd rejoin forces with the other officers, sneak up to the fence and treat the operation like a SWAT takedown.

The sheriff and his team were to set up the perimeter and provide containment, while Christian and his group of Texas Rangers were the entry team. Bright lights and loud noises, then before you could say "Remember the Alamo," the meth-cookers would be in custody. At least that was how it was supposed to happen. Christian would reserve judgment on the merits of the plan until it actually worked.

The *whop-whop* of the helicopter blades echoed off the canyon wall and bounced into the stillness of the evening. It was as dark as Christian imagined hell would be. The only light was the muted blue of the helicopter's instrument panel. And even in the mountain air, the stifling heat inside Christian's Kevlar-and-Nomex uniform created a stream of sweat that ran down his rib cage. Oh, yeah—this had to be hell.

C.J. snapped his gum and idly stroked his MP5. Snap, snap, crackle. It was his way of focusing, but it was driving Christian crazy. Only a few more minutes until the action.

Christian surveyed the boulder-strewn landscape through the surreal green glow of his night-vision goggles as the helicopter put down softly. It was the perfect place for an ambush—by the bad guys.

C.J. apparently recognized the danger, too. "Okay, boss, here goes. You watch my rear and I'll watch yours. It's party time." C.J. was the first man out of the chopper and scrambled away from the backwash of the rotor blade. Christian was right behind him.

It didn't take long to confirm their premonition. No sooner had Christian hit the ground than gunfire exploded around them. Christian dropped to the hard-baked sand and did a quick reconnaissance—and noticed that the rest of the team had correctly assessed the situation and were laying down protective firepower from the chopper.

The *rat-a-tat-tat* of automatic weapons was coming from every direction. The only way they'd get out of there in one piece was the way they came in—on the helicopter. And if the accelerating whine of the engine was any indication, that bird was about to take off.

"C.J., C.J., where are you?" Christian yelled into the headphone. "Get back to the chopper." The sounds and the smells were straight out of Dante's Inferno.

"Sorry, boss, no can do. I've been hit."

"Where are you?" Christian shouted again. He was still on his belly in the swirling dirt. Sticking his head up wasn't an option. But C.J. couldn't be too far away. "How close are you to the door?"

There was a pause. "Ten feet, maybe. Straight out. That guy's about to take off. Leave now!"

Not likely. Bullets ricocheted off the side of the aircraft. But by the grace of God, the bad guys couldn't hit the broad side of a barn. He had three minutes max to find C.J. and throw him on the helicopter, or they'd both be dead.

Christian inched forward on his belly until he saw what he thought was C.J.'s boot. "Kick the dirt!"

C.J. answered with a weak chuckle. "You've always been a sucker for lost causes, haven't ya, boss?"

"Shut up and move your foot!"

Thank God, the foot moved. Christian scooted over to C.J.'s side. He'd make a perfect target when he stood up, but he'd just have to chance that.

Two minutes! The rotor blades whirled faster and faster. Christian lifted C.J. in a fireman's grip and lurched toward the Huey. One minute! The downwash made the ten-foot run feel more like a hundred yards. Thirty seconds! Christian threw C.J. in and jumped behind him just as the helicopter lifted off.

Christian took his friend's hand. "It'll be okay. We'll have you to a hospital before you even know what happened."

C.J. coughed. "That was a real goat rope." Then he passed out.

They finally stopped the flow of blood but it was everywhere—on the floor, on the walls, on his hands and face and clothes. God, a man couldn't live long with that kind of blood loss. The flight to the roof of the large hospital only took thirty minutes, but it felt like a lifetime.

A green-clad emergency-room team met them when they landed. They put C.J. on a gurney and ran toward the elevator, with Christian and his Ranger buddies right behind them. They weren't about to let C.J. out of their sight. Clad in black, smeared in blood and toting MP5 assault rifles, they were an ominous sight. No wonder people scurried out of their way. He'd move if he saw them coming, too.

Everyone scattered except a short, plump woman in green scrubs who stepped in front of them like an irate traffic cop. "You're not going in there. You're filthy and the last thing he needs is an infection." She was adamant. They were *not* entering *her* trauma room.

Christian pulled the satellite phone from his belt. It was time to bring in the resources of the Texas DPS. "Captain, C.J.'s been shot and we need to get him home."

TWELVE HOURS LATER, Christian watched the ambulance crew load C.J. on a Learjet for the trip to San Antonio. He was pale as death and bags of fluids hung off the gurney, but the doc said he thought he'd make it. Christian hopped aboard.

The days of the Texas Republic were numbered. This stuff had to end, and Christian would be right in the middle of the fray. It had gone well beyond getting the Texas Republic fruitcakes out of the picture and their drugs off the streets. It had turned into something extremely personal.

Chapter Thirty

"Chief, you've got a call on line two. It's Lieutenant Delacroix's captain from Houston." Dora's announcement made Lolly's heart beat wildly. At the best of times, a call from Captain Thornton wasn't good, but with Christian and C.J. on a mission, the possibilities were terrifying.

She took a deep breath and picked up the receiver. "This is Chief LaTullipe."

"Chief, Larry Thornton here. I hate to call you like this, but I'm in the air on my way to San Antonio."

Oh, my God! Was it Christian? This was the call she'd dreaded. Through the buzzing in her ears, Lolly realized the captain was still talking.

"C.J. was shot and we're having him air-evaced to San Antonio. They should be landing in about two hours. Thought you'd want to know."

Lolly couldn't utter a word. She took another deep breath. "How is he?"

Captain Thornton paused. "I don't know. Not good. But that's all I can really tell you."

The question she needed to ask was stuck in her throat.

The captain must have been a mind reader, because

he provided the information. "Christian's fine. He's mad, but he's okay."

Lolly's mind was working a mile a minute trying to figure out how to get Olivia to San Antonio—ASAP. It was obvious that Livy was bedazzled, bothered and bewitched by C.J., the most charming rogue in all of south Texas.

"We'll be there in three or four hours. What hospital?"

The captain gave her all the details, and when she hung up her head was spinning. She had to make arrangements to leave the office for a couple of days, then she needed to organize care of the kids, and last but certainly not least, she had to find Olivia. Thanks to Sergeant Joe and Mee Maw, the first two were taken care of quickly, and that left breaking the news to Olivia. Lolly headed to the vet clinic. This couldn't be done over the phone.

The clinic was crowded with pets waiting to see the doc. A socially inept black Lab sniffed Lolly's crotch, as a delusional Yorkie tried to take on a dog five times its size. To make matters worse, a parrot in a large cage screeched periodically.

Lolly spoke to the receptionist. "Hey, Kristin, I have to see Doctor Olivia right away. I think it's better if I talk to her back there." She pushed open the double doors. "This is sort of official business."

Kristin led Lolly to the clinic, where Olivia was scrubbing her hands.

"Lolly! What are you doing here in the middle of the day?" The expression on Lolly's face must have alerted her. "What is it? Is it my dad?"

Lolly put her arm around her friend's shoulders. "No, it's C.J. He was hurt and they're flying him back to San Antonio."

"What? Where? How?"

"The captain called and said he'd been shot. I think it's bad." She was afraid Olivia might faint, but her friend quickly recovered.

"I'm here to take you to the hospital. I packed an overnight bag for you. It's in the car."

Olivia drew in a deep, shuddery breath. "Let me talk to Bob and I'll be ready."

She disappeared down a hallway and reappeared a few minutes later, looking only marginally better. At least she didn't look as if she'd keel over any second.

"How fast can we get there?"

"I have a cruiser. We'll fly." And they did.

LOLLY WHIPPED INTO the staff parking lot—no one would dare ticket a cruiser. Olivia was out of the car and running across the pavement before Lolly could even cut the engine. Getting into ICU was going to be tricky, but if all else failed, Lolly would flash her badge. And if that didn't work, they could fall back on Livy's lab coat and stethoscope.

Lolly caught up with Olivia at the emergency room entrance and grabbed her arm. "Let me take over from here. I'll see if I can pull some strings."

"And if they're not impressed, show them your gun." That was more like the Olivia she knew and loved. She hadn't said a word all the way from Port Serenity, and that quiet white-faced woman was a stranger. Of course, she was probably scared witless from screaming along at a hundred miles per hour for the entire trip.

Apparently a title could open any door, especially if that title happened to be doctor or chief. They were directed upstairs to the intensive-care waiting room, a place normally restricted to family members.

When Lolly and Olivia got off the elevator, she saw Christian in deep conversation with a man wearing a Stetson and toting a big gun—yup, had to be Captain Thornton.

Christian was still dressed in his black BDUs. He had dried blood smears on his forearms and hands, but he was the most gorgeous man Lolly had ever laid eyes on. It took every bit of willpower she possessed not to run over and smother him with kisses. Then she wanted to haul him home and handcuff him to her bed until they were old and gray and too feeble to get into trouble.

Almost before she could step out of the elevator, she was in his arms. He was so big, and solid, and safe. But safety in their business was ephemeral. "How's C.J.?"

"I don't know. He'll be in surgery another couple of hours. We'll have to wait and see. He lost a lot of blood." He pulled Olivia into his arms, too. "Come here."

Lolly didn't know how long they stood there in their own private world of comfort.

"Come over and meet Captain Thornton. He's done everything possible to get C.J. the best care available." Christian drew them over to the tall man with gunmetal-gray hair and kind eyes.

Day melted into night. It was a parody of normal life. Candy bars, inane game shows on a muted TV and family members of other patients wandering in for short visits.

Lolly squirmed on the plastic couch. "You'd think they'd make this place more comfortable, wouldn't you?" They'd been there for hours, and C.J. had just come back from the recovery room. The prognosis was good, but he still wasn't out of danger.

His mother was somewhere in Europe and his brother was a photojournalist on assignment. For the time being, the little group in the waiting room was his family. Lolly hoped that would carry some weight with Nurse Ratchet.

And speaking of the intimidating nurse, there she was in the flesh. "As soon as we get him settled, one of you can come in for fifteen minutes." She frowned. "Fifteen minutes and not a second more."

Olivia spoke to Christian. "You go in first. He'll want to know what happened."

The night was broken only by the fifteen-minute vigils they were allowed in C.J.'s room every hour. Once he was lucid enough to speak to them, shades of his old charm broke through.

Lolly squeezed Livy's hand after she returned from one of the visits. "I'm going across the street to get us a hotel room. Then I'm coming back to get you. You need a shower, a bite to eat and a bed. And I'm not taking no for an answer." She turned to Christian and sniffed. "If I can, I'll get a suite because *you* need a shower."

He chuckled and that was the best sound she'd heard in ages.

The second day at the hospital wasn't much different from the first. Every time Christian went in for his visit, it seemed to him that his friend was getting stronger. He couldn't stand that waiting room. The captain had left for Houston, but before he departed he'd instructed Christian to stay as long as necessary.

At the moment, all he wanted to do was savor the

woman in his arms. Olivia was in C.J.'s room and Lolly was nestled against his chest, not that they could do anything in a waiting room full of distraught family members.

"Do you think he'll be okay?" she mumbled.

"Yeah, I do. On the flight back, I had some doubts, but now I'm sure he's gonna make it. He's one tough cookie." He smiled. "Pun intended. And by the way, I've been wondering how he got the nickname 'Cookie.'"

Lolly snuggled in his arms. "You know how kids are in elementary school—they'll pin a nickname on other kids just to make them crazy. But they never were able to get under C.J.'s skin. I swear, the man would spit at a rattler."

Christian ran his fingers through her hair. "And this time he almost met that rattler face-to-face."

"Olivia's in love with him."

"Yeah, I'm afraid you're right." He frowned at the thought. "And the interesting thing is that it's reciprocated."

Afraid? That was a strange way of putting it. "What's wrong with them loving each other?"

He sat up abruptly, almost dumping her off the couch. "There's something I need to tell you. Then, between the two of us, maybe we can figure out how to tell Olivia."

The expression on his face scared her. What could be that bad? As she heard the elevator door ping, she felt him stiffen.

"Oh, great," he muttered. "I've waited too long."

"Waited too long for what?"

He didn't answer. Instead, he stood, walked over to the stunning young redhead who stepped off the elevator and put his arm around her.

What in the world was happening? Christian kept his arm around the girl while she cried. Lolly knew C.J. didn't have any sisters or cousins, especially ones who looked like *that*. So who was she?

Christian turned toward Lolly and then resumed his conversation with the woman. *Girl* was probably a more apt description—she couldn't be a day over twenty. Their conversation was animated. The woman could have been leading an orchestra the way she was waving her hands.

It seemed like forever, but it was probably just a few minutes before Christian took the girl's elbow and led her over to the seating area.

"Lolly, this is Selena. She's C.J.'s wife," he said hoarsely.

Lolly's mouth dropped open. "*Wife?* What do you mean his wife?" Her voice rose several octaves. "Lord have mercy! What about Olivia?"

And speaking of Olivia, she took that moment to reappear.

"Livy." Lolly tried to put her body between Olivia and the redhead. "Come with me. We need to talk."

"Right now? C.J. just told me he loves me!"

Lolly pulled her friend toward the ladies' room. "Really? That's great." And it didn't mean diddly-squat. "Come with me. Now. It's a matter of life and death." C.J.'s life or death.

Lolly pushed her into the lavatory and plastered herself against the door.

Olivia whirled around. "Okay, Miss Smarty Pants, I'm here. What's so important?"

Lolly searched for someplace private, but the toilet was the only option. She shoved Olivia into the stall. "Sit."

"No!"

She put her hands on Livy's shoulders. "I really think you should. We have to talk."

The serious tone of Lolly's voice must have registered because Olivia stopped protesting. "What's wrong now? Is there a problem at home?"

Lolly crouched in front of her friend. "No, everything at home is fine. It's here that we have a problem." She shook her head. "I don't know how to break this to you, so here goes. I just found out that C.J.'s married. The redhead is his wife."

Olivia was silent for a few minutes and then burst out laughing. "That's a terrible thing to say." She smacked Lolly on the arm. "Married! That's beyond stupid. You *are* kidding, aren't you?" Olivia was working her way to a screech. "Aren't you?"

"No, I'm not kidding."

Under most circumstances, it was fairly difficult to rile Olivia, but this time she was peeved, big-time.

"That no-good scum-sucking pig! I oughta kill him." She beat on the stall door. "I'm going to neuter him. We'll see how he likes being married without the use of the family jewels," she sneered as she paced the small room.

"That's it. I'm outta here." Olivia stormed into the waiting room and came to a halt in front of Selena. "Ha! Jailbait!" She stomped off to the exit stairs with Lolly on her heels.

"Wait." Christian took two strides and grabbed Lolly's arm. "There's something you need to know before you go after her." He gestured in the direction of the stairs.

It was highly doubtful that anything Christian could tell her would change Livy's mind about leaving, or committing murder, or anything else.

The poor man looked like he'd rather be having a root canal without Novocaine. "Technically he's married, but he's not *really* married."

Lolly lifted an eyebrow. "Honestly?"

"God's truth. It's a green-card marriage. C.J. rescued Selena from a really bad situation down in Colombia. You know C.J.—he's always picking up strays." Christian put his hands on Lolly's shoulders. "Believe me, he's not interested in her in any kind of wifely way. He's putting her through college. When she graduates in a couple of months, they're planning to get divorced."

"Truth?"

"Truth. I'd lay my life on it."

"How did she find out about the shooting?" Lolly asked.

"I called her. I didn't think she'd make it down here so soon. She's a good kid, and she loves him like a brother. I thought I'd have more time to explain things before she showed up." Christian sighed. "But I didn't...."

Chapter Thirty-One

Olivia threw another wad of clothes into the duffel bag. "Don't say a word, especially not if you're about to defend that—that turkey."

Lolly raised her hands in surrender. "Not me. We have plenty of time to talk on our way home."

Olivia tossed her toiletries into the bag. "You don't have to leave. I can catch a flight."

"No. Let me get my stuff." Poor, poor C.J.!

It was a long, very silent ride home. Whenever Lolly tried to bring up the subject of C.J., she got the deep freeze. Lordy mercy, the temp outside was hovering near a hundred, and she didn't even need to run the air conditioner, it was so frigid inside the car.

One thing Lolly couldn't tolerate was the silent treatment; and whether she wanted to or not, Doctor Olivia *was* going to listen. She took the exit to Three Rivers and turned into the drive-through for Dairy Queen.

"I am not going to have a chocolate shake and you can't make me." Olivia was wearing the pouty, stubborn look Lolly hated, detested, despised and abhorred.

"Oh, yeah, you are. You'd be surprised what it can cure." Lolly spoke to the girl at the take-out window. "Two large chocolate shakes."

Olivia crossed her arms and slumped in the seat.

Lolly ripped the paper off the straw and jabbed it into the cup. "Drink it!" Then she pulled over. "You're listening—even if I have to pull my gun on you."

She hit the electric locks. "Technically, he's married. But he isn't really married."

Olivia's glare could have melted an iceberg. "Bull puckey."

Lolly took a big slurp of chocolate courage. "Nope. It's true. You're smart. Aren't you the least bit interested in why C.J. would marry a girl that young?" Merciful heavens, Olivia had to be blood kin to a jackass. "And if you stick your fingers in your ears I'm gonna smack you."

Despite her less-than-receptive audience, Lolly told the whole rescue, green card, college story—or as much as she knew, anyway. As she expected, the tale was greeted by dead silence. "Okay, be an idiot, see if I care." Lolly tore out of the parking lot and went back to the freeway. The seventy-five miles to Port Serenity seemed longer than ever before.

It wasn't until she arrived at Olivia's house that the conversation continued.

"I'll concede that what you told me makes sense, considering C.J. He does have a habit of picking up strays." A fat tear rolled down Olivia's face. "He feeds Peachtree all the time. Says he feels sorry for him."

Lolly could see that her friend was weakening. "I don't know if you remember this from high school, but he always befriended the kids everyone else teased. Not many teenagers can make that claim."

"But he didn't tell me. If he had, maybe we could've worked something out. But he didn't. I don't know if I can forgive him."

Lolly unhooked her seat belt to hug her friend. "Promise me you'll keep an open mind. You can't afford to throw love away. None of us can." She wiped the tears from Olivia's face. "You've got time to think about it. He won't be out of the hospital for a while."

Chapter Thirty-Two

To the casual observer, Lolly's life had returned to its usual pace. There was school, football practice and piano lessons. Kids trundled in and out of the house as if it was Times Square on New Year's Eve. Mee Maw was almost back to normal. Lolly hoped it didn't have anything to do with the weird phone calls she'd been getting. Lolly talked to Christian every day. And even though she'd had quite a tussle between heart and head, Lolly was committed to the whole marriage gig with Mr. Wonderful.

C.J. was getting better by leaps and bounds. The man was as stubborn as Olivia and definitely too ornery to die. Everything would be okay.

Christian stood at the screen door and watched her wash the dishes. He remembered the first time he'd watched her at that sink. That was the evening they'd first made love—the evening he'd yearned to touch something kind, and good, and precious.

With a stealth borne of years in the field, he soundlessly moved over and kissed her neck. And for his trouble he got a wet dishrag in the face. She obviously didn't think it was as sexy as he did.

Lolly squealed. "My God! You scared the piddle out of me." She whacked him with the dishrag again.

"Is that any kind of greeting?" he asked as he put his arms around her waist and closed in for a kiss. This encounter wasn't going much further than a stolen kiss—not with most of the freshman football team playing "shirts and skins" in the front yard and at least half a dozen little girls in the tree house.

"Why don't we get Mee Maw to come over and we can go to my place?"

Lolly shook her head. "I can't. Mama and Aunt Sissy are in Corpus. And I've got to fix supper and then go to the Kiwanis barbecue. Lance wants me to promote a bond issue." She reached up on tiptoe to nibble his bottom lip. "But I *can* give you some sugar."

Damn her black heart, the woman knew what she was doing—and what she was doing was making him think about hot nights and rumpled sheets. But two could play at that game.

He feathered his fingers up the tender skin of her inner thigh. A soft sigh escaped her lips.

He slipped his fingers under the hem of her shorts and played with the elastic band of her lacy panties. In one of his few lucid moments, he wondered if they were the peach ones with the matching bra that he liked so much.

"Oh, Christian," she breathed before she nipped his earlobe.

He was about to reach Nirvana when the front door slammed open and the foyer filled with a bunch of teenage boys who smelled like dead fish.

Lolly jumped at least a foot in the air. "Later."

It was amazing—the woman went from precoital ecstasy to no-nonsense mom in 1.5 seconds.

The racket got louder as the boys headed toward the kitchen and the refrigerator.

Lolly stopped Bren before they could deplete her food stores. "How many are staying for supper? We're having burgers."

"Hey, guys! Who wants to have burgers?" Four kids decided that sounded better than anything being served at home.

"You boys take the Cokes and chips outside. We'll have supper in a little bit. And don't pester the girls."

The gang of boys resembled a plague of locusts. They made a lot of noise, stripped the land of food and then, poof—they disappeared.

"Why don't you go out and get the barbecue ready," she said to Christian. "If they ask too many questions, tell them to go away." She knew he wouldn't do that; he was too nice to those kids.

Dinner was another scorched-earth experience. The kids ate like it was a training table for the NFL. Finally, an hour later, all was quiet. The friends went home, the resident kids were in their rooms, and Lolly and Christian were snuggled on the porch swing.

"How's C.J.?"

"He's better. I think he'll be out of the hospital within the week."

She wanted to see his expression when she asked the next question. "And what's happened to his wife?"

"She's in school."

"You know, if C.J. ever expects to get back into Olivia's good graces, he'll have to do a lot of groveling."

"I figured that." Christian tweaked her nose. "You two are hard, hard women."

"And Olivia can be incredibly stubborn."

"So that's why you're such good friends."

She smacked him on the arm and wriggled closer. The steady beat of his heart and the solid strength of his muscles made her feel safe and secure. Even the rumble of his voice was comforting. Until she realized exactly *what* he was saying.

"I know you won't be happy about this, but I'm returning to the Texas Republic compound to finish the job."

Over her dead body! "No way! You're not going back there to get killed. Wasn't it enough that C.J. almost died?"

For heaven's sake, she was a professional peace officer and so was he; hysteria was not an appropriate reaction to this kind of news. But they didn't even know what had caused the last debacle. That just wasn't acceptable.

He tried to comfort her by rubbing her arm, but she slid to the end of the swing.

"Don't touch me. I can't think when you do that."

Christian smiled slyly. "Good." He moved closer so their thighs brushed. "You have to listen to me." He cupped her chin in his hand. "We have a plan, and hopefully nothing will go wrong this time."

"Hopefully, hopefully! Hopefully doesn't hack it," she screeched.

"Lolly, can you hear what you're saying? What if I said you couldn't go out on patrol because it's dangerous? What would you say to that?"

"I'd tell you to go screw yourself. But this is different! There's a good chance you could get killed. And I don't think I could live through that."

"Lolly, Lolly, my love." He kissed her. "I'll be okay. I promise."

It sounded good, but there weren't any guarantees in

life. "And what happens after we get married and you go and get yourself killed? Then what would I do? Tell the kids not to worry that they just lost another daddy? No way! And what about transferring to the desk job? Did you tell me that in order to get me to say yes?"

Oops! She knew the minute the comment was out of her mouth that she'd messed up—royally. She didn't usually get hysterical, but she'd done a bang-up job this time.

His chest didn't feel so snuggly anymore. In fact, it felt like a board. He was still as death, and when he spoke she could feel the acid dripping off each word.

"What do you mean by that comment?" His words were soft and deadly in their precision.

If all else failed, a good offense was the best defense. "I mean that if you're planning to go off willy-nilly to get shot at by every slime-bag drug dealer in North America, maybe I don't want to get married to you. I need someone with a sense of responsibility."

Double oops.

When he stood up, she almost fell off the swing. "In that case, why don't you just keep the ring or sell it and buy a riding lawn mower. Frankly, I don't care." He marched off the porch without a backward look. Rhett Butler couldn't have done it better. The last thing she saw was the taillights of his car as he rounded the corner.

She'd really screwed up. And the chances of being forgiven were probably slim to none—and slim had left town.

Chapter Thirty-Three

Captain Thornton leaned back in the big leather chair, his boots planted on top of his desk. "Brief me on everything you know about these Texas Republic guys."

Christian drew a hand down his face. Ever since his blowup with Lolly he'd felt like the bottom of an outhouse. Sleep was minimal, eating was only on an as-needed basis and he'd do just about anything to avoid thinking. If he'd only kept his cool, they could have worked things out. But no, he had to get macho and tell her to cram the ring.

But if he intended to prove her wrong and come home alive, he had to put every bit of his focus on this mission. "One of the sleaziest guys north of the border is my informant. He lives in Fort Stockton, but his brother is out in Sierra Blanca. The brother says he can get into the compound and give us the location of the two head honchos—they're cousins. The plan is to keep it simple. A couple of Texas Rangers and I will sneak in and haul their rotten butts out in the middle of the night. Then everything should fall apart."

The captain nodded and let Christian continue with

his briefing. "You trust these Rangers? We don't want another C.J. situation."

"Absolutely."

The captain shook his head. "At least we've discovered how the bad guys were getting their information. Just as we suspected… I'd like to string up that dirty deputy by his privates. A cop like that makes me want to puke!"

Christian's sentiments exactly.

"So you're *sure* this guy will give you good information?" Thornton asked.

"Yep, I think so, for the right amount of money. I'm heading out west in the morning. My Texas Ranger buddies are anxious to start the ball rolling."

The captain looked at Christian with laser precision. "Be careful. Now get out of here and do what you have to do." He paused. "When you're done there's a desk job waiting for you."

THE INTERIOR OF the cantina was dark and smelled of sweat, urine and years of spilled tequila. An unidentified object crunched under Christian's foot as he walked toward the bar. They should probably rename the place La Cucaracha.

Several customers put down their drinks and stared. In this crowd, anyone unfamiliar posed a threat. It took a few minutes for his eyes to adjust to the gloom; then he saw his contact. The guy had his back to the wall and was talking to a Charles Manson look-alike.

Christian had been sucked into the underbelly of society once again, dealing with men who would sell out their mothers for a few bucks. Thank God this was his last undercover assignment. He was going home, and by hook or crook, he was going to win the woman he loved.

But for now, he had a job to do. Christian joined the men and ordered a beer. He, too, kept his back to the wall. "Can you pinpoint the exact location of the leaders? No screwups?"

His Fort Stockton connection rubbed his fingers together in the international sign for money. "Sure, with the right incentive."

"Name it."

And when he did, Christian nodded. It was cheaper than he'd budgeted. Nothing on heaven or earth was going to keep him from taking out the jerks from the so-called Texas Republic.

CHRISTIAN WAS slithering across a rock-strewn landscape on his belly. The night was as black as sin—even the stars had taken a hike—but the sounds of the desert were myriad. The skittering noise of scorpions. The hiss of a sidewinder as it evaded the three-man team intent on finishing their mission before the sun streaked across the eastern sky.

A razor-wire fence loomed ahead. Good, his informant hadn't failed him. Now, they just had to overpower the guards and snatch the drug kingpins. If God was in his heaven, this operation would come off with a minimum of screwups.

"There's a dude at twelve o'clock," he whispered over the radio to his Texas Ranger colleagues. It wasn't like working with C.J. They were as close as brothers, they almost breathed in unison. But these guys were the best. And that was a damned good thing, since he was betting his life on their expertise.

A slight noise came from the spot where the guard had been standing. "I got him," the Ranger whispered. "He's down for the count. Ready?"

"Yeah," Christian muttered, leading the way into the compound. If everything went according to plan, the ringleaders would be handcuffed and in the back of a squad car before the rest of their gang knew what had happened.

Christian slipped into the bedroom of his assigned target. He plunged the syringe of sedative into the bad guy's bare arm. The subject made a few muffled groans, then went dead still. Christian picked him up in a fireman's hold and crept outside.

"I got mine. Meet you at the spot." A couple of sheriff's deputies were stationed beyond the perimeter fence to assist in the arrest.

It was just as well he'd be leaving this stuff to the young guys. Imagine that—thirty-five and he was getting too old! It wasn't the physical nature of the job; it was more that the fire in his belly had died down.

Time to go home and convince his woman to take pity on him.

Groveling loomed large in his future.

Chapter Thirty-Four

Lolly twirled the large square diamond on her left finger. Why hadn't she taken the darn thing off? She was in the middle of a wonderful pity party and it would take too much energy—that was why.

"Isn't that right, Harvey?" The lazy mound of fur thumped his tail in agreement.

Lolly was about to scoop another spoonful of Ben & Jerry's Chocolate Fudge Brownie out of the container when the back door creaked. It had better be a friend!

"Lolly, where are you?"

Livy. Terrific, just terrific! Not that she didn't enjoy Olivia's company; but a blue funk was solitary entertainment, not a party game.

Lolly didn't move from her spot on the floor. "In the living room."

"What in the world are you doing in here? Other than having a chocolate orgy." Olivia gestured at the food on the floor and the coffee table.

"What was your first clue? The Snickers, the brownies or the Ben & Jerry's?" Lolly held up the pint of ice cream. "Pull up a cushion and sit down." Lolly pushed Harvey's prone body aside to make room. "I'm bingeing, so hush up and join me." She handed Olivia a plate of brownies. "Mee Maw made them." No matter how bad the situation got, Mee Maw's brownies always came to the rescue.

Olivia popped a chocolate morsel in her mouth and sighed. "Okay, tell Auntie Livy what's up. You haven't done this since you found Wendell with his drawers down."

"Oh, Livy," she wailed. "My babies are growing up. They're never home. They're always going here, there and everywhere. My mother has a broken heart and she's been acting really weird. Plus, the man I love is...is—whatever." She threw her hands in the air. "And I haven't taken this *ring* off."

Olivia grabbed the spoon and ice cream carton away from her friend. "At least he's not married. Now *that's* a bummer. Not to mention the fact that he fell off the planet the minute he left the hospital."

"You mean C.J. hasn't called you?"

"Nope. Not a word."

Lolly dug out a huge spoonful of chocolate. She didn't know whether to tell her friend what she'd heard, but finally decided Olivia deserved the truth. "Rumor has it that C.J.'s resigned from the DPS. He's going to take a job as a sheriff's deputy in Aransas County."

Livy scowled fiercely. "That bottom-feeding slug. He's coming home and didn't bother to even let me know!" she screeched. "I'm going to shoot him, but first I'm gonna neuter him." Olivia ate a mini-Snickers and snorted. "Boy, is that sucker going to have an un-pleasant welcoming party. No one messes with Olivia Alvarado and gets away with it."

Lolly muted the TV. Poor C.J. "Have some more

chocolate. It'll make you feel better." Too bad she didn't have any Valium to offer her friend.

"Hmph!"

"Seriously, it will."

Olivia stuck another chocolate nugget in her mouth. "Okay, Mama." She smiled a smile of pure devilment. "I'll get over this—just as soon as I get even."

Oh, poor, poor C.J.!

"On to another subject, I came over to watch 'the show' with you." Olivia made quotation marks with her fingers.

That was a topic Lolly would rather skip. Two weeks before, the film crew from *America's Most Wanted* had arrived on her doorstep to feature the Twisted Oaks gang.

Olivia scooped up the remote. "There you are."

Sure enough, Lolly was being interviewed. She had watched the actors film the piece, but now it seemed surreal. It all came home to roost when they flashed her former friends' pictures and descriptions on the screen.

Olivia stared at the TV. "They're toast."

Yep—they were toast! Unless they were at some secret compound in the mountains of Mexico as Aunt Sissy had hinted. Then all bets were off. And to top it all, the ditzy twins, Mee Maw and Aunt Sissy, were planning a trip south of the border. They said they were going shopping—yeah, right!

"That's it." Olivia yanked the sack of Snickers bars away and threw it on the table. "If you don't stop eating, your butt's gonna look like two boar hogs in a sack. Get dressed. We're going out." Olivia stood up and pulled Lolly with her.

"I don't want to go out. I want to stay here and wallow."

"No wallowing allowed." She snapped the elastic

waistband of Lolly's sweatpants. "Go change into something sexy. Now."

Olivia had on her obstinate look so Lolly shuffled off to change. Better to give in now than wage the battle and lose the war. "I'm not wearing anything sexy. I'm done with sexy. I think I might join a convent."

"You're not Catholic. You have to be Catholic to be a nun."

Lolly put her hands on her hips, then ruined the effect by giggling. "I'll start a new trend. I'll be a Baptist nun."

"Go change," Olivia demanded and pointed toward the bedroom. It took only a few minutes for Lolly to throw on a T-shirt and jeans.

She was in Livy's car before she had the presence of mind to ask where they were going. Entertainment opportunities were fairly limited in Port Serenity at this time of year. She wrapped her arms around her middle. All that chocolate was making her queasy.

"Where are we headed?"

"You'll see when we get there," Olivia said with a smirk.

What was she up to now?

Lolly found out when they pulled into the parking lot of the Peaceful Cove Inn. She crossed her arms over her chest.

"Nope. I'm not going in there. No way, no how."

"Aw, come on. We'll have a couple of beers and a game of pool. Be a sport."

"Nope! I don't want a beer and I don't know how to shoot pool. And if a Bubba tries to pinch my butt, I'll shoot him. Then I'd lose my job and my kids wouldn't be able to go to college." Lolly frowned. "So, no—I won't go in there."

"For pity's sake." Olivia exited the car and came around to the passenger side. "If you don't get out, I'm going to drag you out."

"Hmph!"

"Yeah, hmph." Olivia jerked the door open. "Out!"

Lolly knew she'd never win the argument so she followed Olivia into the dark reaches of the bar. It looked and smelled just like the last time she was in there—when she first encountered Christian.

Lolly reluctantly sidled up to the bar. No kidding, if one of the cretins even dared lay a finger on her derriere, they were dead meat.

Bud plopped two beers on the bar. "Ain't seen you around here lately, Chief."

And if she was lucky he wouldn't see her much in the future, either. "No, I've been busy with the summer crowd and everything." Falling in love and being an idiot took time and energy.

Olivia pointed toward a dim corner. "There's a table over there."

It was so darn dark she couldn't see at all. The candles on the tables and the light over the pool table provided the only illumination.

Lolly was stumbling along when a large male arm grabbed her. Next thing she knew, she was in his lap, plastered up against his chest. Where was her stun gun when she needed it?

"Don't even consider it, darlin'," he whispered.

She knew that voice and she knew that chest. In fact, she was intimately acquainted with the whole body. She stiffened and then whirled to go nose-to-nose with Christian. "What *do* you think you're doing?"

He ran his fingers through her hair and drew her

mouth down to his. "I think I'm kissing you." And that's what he did, with relish.

When Lolly could catch her breath, she realized she'd been reeled in like a great big old catfish. But she couldn't be too mad at either of the conspirators.

"You knew he was going to be here, didn't you?" she asked her friend.

Olivia had the temerity to look innocent. It might have worked, but then she giggled. "I'm going to leave you lovebirds to have a talk. I'll be over there playing pool if you need me." She strolled off without a backward glance.

Christian cupped Lolly's chin and ran his thumb over the softness of her lower lip. "Are you still mad at me?"

How could she be mad at him? It had taken a lot of soul-searching, but she'd finally seen the light. What he did for a living didn't matter. She could get hit by lightning or beaned by a falling satellite. She wore a gun and a badge, and if that didn't make *her* a target for the bad guys, Lolly didn't know what did. For all she cared, he could go into TEWB wrestling, or bull riding or remain a narc cop. Whatever he decided to do was fine with her. She wanted him in her life—for now and forever.

Lolly ran her fingers over the bristly stubble on his cheeks. "I wasn't mad at you, I was being an idiot."

"Really?"

"Really."

Christian played with the diamond ring on her left hand. "You didn't take it off." He picked up her hand and kissed her palm. "I hope that means you'll reconsider marrying me."

She almost knocked him off the chair when she threw herself at him and twined her arms around his neck.

"Oh, yes. Definitely yes. You're stuck with me for the rest of your life. I love you."

He had died and gone to heaven. He was going to grow old with the woman he loved. What a lucky man— he'd snagged the sexiest, most lovable woman in the entire world and she'd given him a ready-made family complete with two great kids, a big goofy dog, cats *and* a white picket fence.

Life just didn't get any better than that.

Welcome to the world of American Romance!
Turn the page for excerpts from our August
2005 titles.

A FABULOUS WIFE
by Dianne Castell

JUDGING JOSHUA
by Mary Anne Wilson

HOMEWARD BOUND
by Marin Thomas

THE ULTIMATE TEXAS BACHELOR
by Cathy Gillen Thacker

We're sure you'll enjoy every one of these books!

A FABULOUS WIFE
by Dianne Castell

A FABULOUS WIFE is the first of three
humorous books about three women in
Whistlers Bend, Montana, who are turning forty
and how they're dealing—or not dealing—
with it. You'll love this new miniseries from
Dianne Castell, called FORTY & FABULOUS.

Watch for A FABULOUS HUSBAND,
coming in October.

Sweat beaded across Jack Dawson's forehead. His stomach clenched. The red LCD numbers on the timer clocked backward. Thirty seconds to make up his mind before this son of a bitch blew sky-high…taking the First National Bank of Chicago and him along for the ride.

What the hell was he doing here? Forty-one was too old for this. He was a detective, a hostage negotiator, not a damn bomb expert…except when the bomb squad got caught in gridlock on Michigan Avenue and the hostage was an uptown financial institution.

He thought of his son graduating…by the sheer grace of a benevolent God…next week in Whistlers Bend, Montana. He couldn't miss that. Maggie would be there, of course. Had it really been ten years since he'd seen his ex? She hated his being a cop. *At the moment he wasn't too thrilled about it, either.*

He remembered Maggie's blue eyes. Maybe it was time for a change.

Always cut white? He held his breath, muttered a prayer, zeroed in on the blue wire…and cut.

JUDGING JOSHUA
by Mary Anne Wilson

In Mary Anne Wilson's four-book series, **RETURN TO SILVER CREEK,** *various characters return to a small Nevada town for a variety of reasons—to hide, to come home, to confront their pasts. In this second book, police officer Joshua Pierce finds himself back in the hometown he was desperate to escape—and is now unable to leave.*

Going back to Silver Creek, Nevada, should have been a good thing. But going home was hard on Joshua Pierce.

He stepped out of the old stone-and-brick police station and into the bitter cold of November. The brilliance of the sun glinting off the last snowfall made him narrow his eyes as he shrugged into his heavy green uniform jacket. Even though he was only wearing a white T-shirt underneath, Joshua didn't bother doing it up as he headed for the closest squad car in the security parking lot to the side of the station.

Easing his six-foot frame into the cruiser, he turned on the motor and flipped the heater on high, waiting for warmth. Two months ago he'd been in the humid heat of an Atlanta September, without any thoughts of coming home. Then his world shifted, the way it had over a year ago, but this time it was his father who needed him.

He pushed the car into gear, hit the release for the security gate, then drove out onto the side street. He was back in Silver Creek without any idea what he'd do when he left here again. And he *would* leave. After all, this wasn't home anymore. For now he was filling in for his father, taking life day by day. It worked. He made it to the next day, time and time again. And that was enough for him, for now.

He turned north on the main street, through the center of a valley framed by the rugged peaks of the Sierra Nevadas soaring into the heavy gray sky to the west and east. Here, some of the best skiing in the west had been a guarded secret for years. Then the word got out, and Silver Creek joined the skiing boom.

The old section of town looked about the same, with stone-and-brick buildings, some dating back to the silver strike in the 1800s. Though on the surface this area seemed like a relic from the past, if you looked more closely, the feed store was now a high-end ski-equipment shop and the general store had been transformed into a trendy coffee bar and specialty cookie store.

Some buildings were the same, such as Rusty's Diner and the Silver Creek Hotel. But everything was changing—even in Silver Creek, change was inevitable. You couldn't fight it, he thought as he drove farther north, into the newer section of town where the stores were unabashedly expensive. He'd tried to fight the changes in his life—all his life—but in the end, he hadn't been able to change a thing. Which is why he was now back in Silver Creek and would be leaving again, sooner or later.

He could only hope it would be sooner.

HOMEWARD BOUND
by Marin Thomas

*Marin Thomas hails from the Dairy State—
Wisconsin—but Texas is now home. It's a good
thing, because there is never a shortage of
cowboys—and never a shortage of
interesting men to write about,
as* HOMEWARD BOUND *shows!*

"Just like old times, huh, Heather?"

The beer bottle halfway to Heather Henderson's mouth froze. Her heart thumped wildly and her muscles bunched, preparing her body for flight. If the voice belonged to whom she assumed, then she was in big trouble.

Longingly, she eyed the bottle in her hand—her first alcoholic drink in over two months, and she hadn't even gotten to take a sip—then lowered it and wiggled it against her Hawaiian skirt. After sucking in a deep breath, she slowly turned and faced her past.

Oh, my.

At six feet two inches, minus the black Stetson, the mayor of Nowhere, Texas, didn't exactly blend in with the gaggle of bikini-clad college coeds in her dorm celebrating end-of-year finals—luau-style. Even if he exchanged his Western shirt, Wranglers and tattered cowboy boots for a pair of swim trunks, he wouldn't fit in—not with his stony face and grim personality. "Hello, Royce. Your timing is impeccable…as usual."

Eyes dark as chunks of coal stared solemnly at her from under the brim of his seen-better-days cowboy hat. His eyes shifted to the bottle peeking out from under her costume, and his mouth twisted into a cynical frown. "Some people never change.... Still the party queen, Heather?"

Obviously he believed she'd held a bottle of beer in her hand more than a textbook since enrolling in college four years ago. She hated the way he always assumed the worst of people. Then again, maybe he was right—some people never changed. *He* appeared to be the same brooding, arrogant know-it-all she remembered from her teen years.

"I'm almost twenty-three." She lifted her chin. "Last time I checked, the legal drinking age in Texas was twenty-one."

His gaze roamed the lobby. "I suppose all these students are twenty-one?"

Rolling her eyes, she snapped, "I see you haven't gotten rid of that trusty soapbox of yours."

The muscle along his jaw ticked and anger sparkled in his eyes—a sure sign he was gearing up for an argument. She waited for her body to tense and her stomach to twist into a knot, but surprisingly, a tingle skittered down her spine instead, leaving her breathless and perplexed.

Shaking off the weird feeling, she set her hands on her hips. "So what if we're breaking the no-alcohol-in-the-dorm rule? No one's in danger of getting written up."

"Just how do you figure that?" he asked.

THE ULTIMATE TEXAS BACHELOR
by Cathy Gillen Thacker

*Welcome back to Laramie, Texas, and
a whole new crop of cowboys!
Cathy Gillen Thacker's new series*
THE McCABES: NEXT GENERATION
*evolved from her popular American Romance
series* THE McCABES OF TEXAS.
*Read this first book of the three, and find out
why this author is a favorite among American
Romance readers!*

"Come on, Lainey. Have a heart! You can't leave us like this!" Lewis McCabe declared as he pushed his eyeglasses farther up on the bridge of his nose.

Besides the fact she was here under false pretenses—which she had quickly decided she couldn't go through with, anyway—Lainey Carrington didn't see how she could stay, either. The Lazy M ranch house looked like a college dorm room had exploded on moving day. Lewis needed a lot more than the live-in housekeeper he had been advertising for to bring order to this mess.

"What do you mean *us?*" she asked suspiciously. Was Lewis married? If so, she hadn't heard about it, but then she hadn't actually lived in Laramie, Texas, since she had left home for college ten years before.

The door behind Lainey opened. She turned and darn near fainted at the sight of the man she had secretly come here to track down.

Not that she had expected the six-foot-three cowboy with the ruggedly handsome face and to-die-for body to actually be here. She had just hoped that Lewis would give her a clue where to look so that she might help her friend Sybil Devine hunt down the elusive Brad

McCabe and scrutinize the sexy Casanova celebrity in person. "Brad, of course, who happens to be my business partner," Lewis McCabe explained.

"Actually, I'm more of a ranch manager," Brad McCabe corrected grimly, shooting an aggravated look at his younger brother. He knocked some of the mud off his scuffed brown leather boots, then stepped into the interior of the sprawling half-century-old ranch house. "And I thought we had an agreement, Lewis, that you'd let me know when we were going to have company so I could avoid running into 'em."

Lewis shot Lainey an apologetic glance. "Don't mind him. He's been in a bad mood ever since he got done filming that reality TV show."

Lainey took this opportunity to gather a little background research. "Guess it didn't exactly have the happily-ever-after ending everyone expected it to have," she observed.

Brad's jaw set. Clearly he did not want her sympathy. "You saw it?"

Obviously he wished she hadn't. Lainey shrugged, not about to admit just how riveted she'd been by the sight of Brad McCabe on her television screen. "I think everyone who knows you did."

"Not to mention most of America," Lewis chimed in.

Bachelor Bliss had pulled in very high ratings, especially at the end, when it had taken an unexpected twist. The success wasn't surprising, given how sexy Brad had looked walking out of the ocean in only a pair of swim trunks that had left very little to the imagination when wet.

"You shouldn't have wasted your time watching such bull," Brad muttered, scowl deepening as his voice dropped a self-deprecating notch. "And I know I shouldn't have wasted mine filming it."

Lainey agreed with him wholeheartedly there. Going on an artificially romantic TV show was no way to find a mate. "For what it's worth, I don't think they did right by you," Lainey continued.

She had heard from mutual acquaintances that Brad McCabe's experience as the sought-after bachelor on *Bachelor Bliss* had turned him into not just a persona non grata where the entire viewing public was concerned, but also into a hardened cynic. That assumption seemed to be true, judging by the scowl on his face and the unwelcoming light in his eyes as he swept off his straw cowboy hat and ran his fingers through his gleaming dark brown hair.

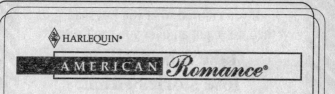

HARLEQUIN®

AMERICAN *Romance*®

is delighted to bring you four new books
in a miniseries by popular author

Mary Anne Wilson

RETURN TO
*Silver
Creek*

In this small town in the high mountain country of
Nevada, four lucky bachelors find love where they
least expect it. And learn you can go home again.

DISCOVERING DUNCAN
On sale April 2005

JUDGING JOSHUA
On sale August 2005

*Available wherever
Harlequin books are sold.*

is happy to bring you
a new 3-book series by

Dianne Castell

Forty & Fabulous

Here are three very funny books
about three women who have grown up
together in Whistler's Bend, Montana.
These friends are turning forty and are
struggling to deal with it. But who said
you can't be forty and fabulous?

A FABULOUS WIFE
(#1077, August 2005)

A FABULOUS HUSBAND
(#1088, October 2005)

A FABULOUS WEDDING
(#1095, December 2005)

Available wherever Harlequin books are sold.